I0674800

Marshwrack

Mark Raney

ISBN: 978-0-578-02136-2

To Peter Owen Bannon
Good Friend, Great Cheerleader, And One Hell Of a Television
News Anchor

All of you will be as dead and lifeless as the washed up marshwrack

CHAPTER ONE

My full name is Benjamin Farrow Meekins. But everyone calls me Ben. Ben is a simple name, but it is also a strong name and a proud name. And now and then I like to say Benjamin Farrow Meekins, outloud to myself to remind myself of the whole lot of history and whole lot of tradition that is in those names. Especially so here on Hatteras. But on Ocracoke as well. Just listing each of the Farrows and each of the Meekins and who they were and what they did during their lifes down through the generations tells much of the history and the tradition of these Outer Banks. So, yes, I do feel good about what has been passed on to me through the name Farrow and through the name Meekins. And Benjamin is a familiar and a trusted first name through much of this history also. So my full name is Benjamin Farrow Meekins. But everyone calls me Ben.

The sea washed up the first shipwrecked ones of both my families onto these Banks so long ago that no one now can trace back to exactly when. Especially my Father's family, the Meekins. Because the Meekins had already long been here on Hatteras when the list of who lived where and who owned what was first made. In fact, the later boats that came searching for what happened to the Lost Colony almost certainly had a Meekins on one of them. So, yes, we Meekins really do go way back to the white mans' beginning here on these Banks. And that is, indeed, a whole lot of history and a whole lot of tradition to be passed along and along and along to me now. Because we men Meekins have always sought the sea. And, whatever her mood and whatever her temper, we men Meekins have never refused the sea.

But my Mother's family, the Farrows, is the more mysterious of the two families. Those who spend time tracing such things think that the first Farrow washed up when a cargo of Egyptian horses shipwrecked north of Hatteras in the seventeen thirties. So the people wily called the nameless castaway hostler who came half drowned among them, Pharaoh, which when written as pronounced became Farrow. And the Farrows that resulted from that first one settled first around Kinnakeet more as merchants than as fishermen before spreading all along these banks and beyond. But strangely the Farrows have always been even more blonde haired and blue-eyed than the Meekins. Rather than the dark-haired and dark-eyed that you would expect. So who knows? And does it matter?

But when a people come to settle to live their history on far removed sand islands, right away they forfeit many of the alternatives for the feeding and the clothing and the sheltering of themselves and of theirs. Because then the sea has quickly gone from just another resource to the only resource. Until there is only the going to sea, and the commerce that is behind that going to sea. And along and along and along, we Meekins mostly went to sea. While we Farrows mostly did the commerce of that going to

5

sea.

So the industry of fishing the whichever resource of whichever season from spring to summer to fall to winter and again and again is all I have ever known. And it is all I have ever done. And it is all I know how to do. So naturally, it has never occurred to me to do anything else. Or even to want to do anything else. And my life would become aimless and useless and senseless if I could never again go fishing. As would my older Brothers' life. And as would my Fathers' life. Because we are fishermen. And that is that. This isolated and special world of boats and gear and engines and nets, and wind and storm and sun and heat and tides and cold. This harsh and demanding world of the hunt and harvest, and the everything that can go wrong and usually does. This very personal world of the freedom to go fishing whenever you want, and the freedom to return from fishing whenever you want, and the freedom to remain at fishing for as long as it suits you. Yes, this world of all the freedom that a man could ever ever hope for.

We live in the two story frame house with the widow-walk that my Grandfather Lemeual Meekins built in the village of Atlantic here on the mainland, soon after he married my Grandmother Sophie Winberry, and not long after he had fled from the ever increasing Meekins crowd crush on Hatteras while still a young man. The Winberry men having long been serious bay scollopers, and I mean serious bay scollopers, down around Bogue Sound near Swansboro and up at southern Core Sound near Harkers Island. But not many years later, as so often happens with men and boats and their fate at sea, Grandfather Lemeual was killed at the wheel of his landing vessel full of Marines at the beach on Tennian in the Pacific. And that was that for Grandfather Lemeual. That he married Grandmother Sophie. That he built this house. That they had my Father. And that he did not refuse the sea. So the history and the tradition was continued.

This house that so dominated the village then. And pretty much still dominates it today. Which, from the second story you can see across the narrow here Core Sound to Portsmouth Island that becomes Core Banks there south of Drum Inlet which never has been much of an ocean inlet for boats that anyone can remember. And from the first story, with the house having been built on brick piers several feet above the sandy soil in case of storm serge flooding, you can see what little there has ever been of the main street businesses of Atlantic. There is the combination grocery store and hardware store. And the combination drug store and restaurant. And the combination filling station and marina behind, with the long dock space for the many work boats whose numbers are decreasing as well as the few pleasure boats whose numbers are increasing.

So from the first story, we can keep up with who is coming and going in the village, as well as what they are wearing. Which is of special interest to my Grandmother and to my Mother and to my younger Sister. And from the second story, we can keep up with who is coming and going in boats on Core Sound, as well as what the weather and the wind and the tide are doing. Which is of special interest to my Father and to my older Brother and to me.

But we have been having our own mini Meekins crowd crush here even in such a large house. But my older Brother will marry Lorena Midgett this summer. And they will live in a house on Cedar Island which is just up the road aways. And that will reduce the Meekins crowd crush here considerably. And I have been hearing my suitcase shuffling itself there under my bed for awhile now. And my going somewhere else for awhile will reduce the Meekins crowd crush here substantially.

We own two fifty some feet wood trawlers which are the pride of the family. And we like to think the pride of the local fishing fleet as well. The Betty Fagan is named for Mom, and Dad is her Captain. And the Mary Margaret is named for my younger Sister, and my older Brother Tommy is her Captain. This while I mate on one trawler or the other trawler, and now and then Captain one trawler or the other trawler, and in general am wherever and whenever I am needed. We are shrimp fishermen, for the most part, and we shrimp the channels of the shallows of Core Sound during spring and summer when the shrimp nursery there. Then we gradually move north during fall to Pamplico Sound as the cold comes and the shrimp move to the deeper warmer water there. During the really harsh months of January and February and March, when the shrimp have gone to sea to spawn, we switch to flounder trawls because the flounder school in the Pamplico Sound then. So for those months we are flounder fishermen. But by April the cycle begins all over again. And so do we. And this has been our life for as long as I can remember. The hunt and the harvest and the weather and the trawlers, and the everything that can go wrong and usually does.

But Dad can remember when shrimp were just a nuisance bycatch that they could not give away except as bait. That was when trout and spot and mullet and croaker and flounder were king. Then suddenly the inlanders finally discovered shrimp, and it became king and it still is king and it probably always will be king now. So we have talked about getting a third trawler for me to Captain. But our total catches have been gradually decreasing in recent years because of over fishing by too many trawlers already. This while the rules and regulations that we must work by have been increased drastically by the Government and this will only worsen. So now Dad says that a third trawler may not be the smart way for us to go. Because Dad and Moms' Brother, Pharaoh Farrow, have been talking about buying some waterfront land down at Sealevel, which is the next village south, and building a dock there as well as a packing and handling building. As well as buying a refrigerated truck so we can sell our catches directly to the northern markets, and there by cut out several middlemen. When that happens then the Betty Fagan will be mine to Captain. Because then Dad will have to spend most of his time at the new facility. Because as Dad says, when Pharaoh Farrow sharpens his pencil, like all the Farrow merchant men before him, one of us Meekins had better be there to watch closely to make certain that Pharaoh isn't sharpening the pencil just for the Farrows. But Dad doesn't say that when Mom is anywhere around.

But all that will not be for awhile yet. Meanwhile, there is the matter of my shuffling itself suitcase to attend to.

CHAPTER TWO

But you have been homesick for home and her people for the several months that you have been here in Georgia. And it is stronger on some days than it is on other days. But it is there to some intensity every day. So it is the last thing you know at night, and it is the first thing you know in the morning. Because everything here has a newness that is much too old. As well as a difference that has long lost its freshness. A place where sullen suspicion somehow is the first reaction to a far more basic fear and distrust toward strangers and change. But no sooner is it clearly there, then it is no longer clearly there. Until, still unable to define it or to describe it, precisely, you question whether you are imagining it. But then, deep inside, you know that you are not.

And this is made worse because it is late summer now, and the shrimp fishing is almost to the point of futility. The early summer good white shrimp run has long been over. Then the mid summer brown shrimp run started well, only to slow, then to trickle, then to become hardly worth the effort. So it will not be until the fall white shrimp run before there is even a hope of making good money again. So until then you can only hang on and hold on physically and emotionally and financially. Because you cannot catch shrimp while tied to the dock. And if you don't go, you don't know. And dogged persistence pays. At least sometimes it does, but not always. So this is called scraping and scrounging for something like a decent paycheck every week. Because there is the same amount of fuel burned, and the same amount of wear and tear to the trawler and to her gear, whether shrimp are caught or not. And these expenses are paid first. And your crew share comes from what is left. If there is anything left.

"Haven't you headed those few shrimp yet?" Now he is standing right behind you. But you didn't hear him walk up what with the heavy loud throb of the engine all around above and below here on the sterndeck. And with your having been lost in homesickness again as well. As you looked long across the wake, and across the wide brown marsh to the far treeline of the highlands where the sun has begun to settle.

"Just go back to driving the boat where you belong, Forrest. I didn't give you permission to come back here." And you are sitting on an overturned five gallon bucket, and the remainder of the last trawl is between and in front of your spread legs in a scattered pile of some of about everything that swims in coastal waters.

"All you Carolina boys have smart mouths. I've noticed that about y'all."

"North Carolina man, not Carolina boy. Don't lump me with those sorry excuses from South Carolina."

"I've never been able to tell the difference. Twiddle de dum and twiddle de dee as far as I'm concerned."

"Well, you Georgia boys can't tell your asses from holes in the ground anyway. I've noticed that about y'all. But you better concern yourself with getting forward and driving this boat before we nose into that mudbank there. I sure don't want to spend half the night out here waiting for the next tide to float us off, just because you didn't do your job."

"Worry about getting those shrimp headed and the trash shoved overboard and the deck washed down before we dock, Ben. That's all you have to worry about."

"Well, you worry about putting us on some shrimp tomorrow. That's your job. I'll do my job. But I'm tired of busting ass every day in this heat for a handfull. You're supposed to be top shrimper around here. But you sure haven't shown me much so far, Forrest. In North Carolina we wouldn't even leave the dock for no more shrimp than we've been getting lately."

"Wait a minute." Then he is forward. Then Mustangs' bow moves from pointing directly at the mudbank at the marsh, and is again pointing up the Intercoastal Waterway. Ahead is the mouth of the creek that winds itself through the wide marsh to the dock that is in the now shadows of the setting sun at the treeline of the highlands now that the summer days have just begun to shorten into fall.

"Okay. So if you want to do it like in North Carolina, then go your ass right on back to North Carolina. Just get your gear and head on up there anytime you want, Ben, if you don't like how I Captain. No one asked you to come here. Strikers are a dime a dozen. I've had a hundred before like you, and I'll have a hundred after you. So you aren't doing me any favor. And I've had all of your smart mouth I'm going to take."

"Just put us on shrimp tomorrow, Forrest. That's all. If you can't, I can. I was born on a shrimp boat just like you."

"I own Mustang, and I'm Captain! We do things my way! And if you don't have that, Ben, you damn well better get that!"

"Look, with fuel and expenses, it looks like I'm going to wind up owing you money again this week. All for the pleasure of busting my ass out here in this heat every day." And in the rush of the argument, you have the last of the shrimp headed and the trash fish and the crabs and the other sea creatures shoved overboard and are now washing down the deck with the hose. "If the shrimp aren't here, then let's go where they are. Off Charleston, off St. Augustine, wherever they are. Anywhere but here. Maybe the important thing to you is to be home every night so you can pat Johanna on the ass, but I'm down here to make money."

"I worry about Johannas' ass, you hear!? You don't worry about Johannas' ass. You got that!? I worry about the where we shrimp and the when we shrimp. You worry about the nets and this deck. That's what you worry about. And that's all you have to worry about. You got that!?"

"You better get forward, Forrest. We've passed the creek."

So Forrest turns Mustang around, then heads her into the winding creek. And the sun is setting more quickly now. So the evening shadows are lengthening and darkening more quickly also. And you can see the bare bulb light at the dock there way across the marsh. And you can smell the thick sweet marsh smells that thicken and sweeten even more at night. And one by one the house lights of the scattered houses in the treeline come on and twinkle in the quickly closing distance. And the stars that are now everywhere overhead have become quite definite. Then a blue heron suddenly rises in loud squacking flight from the mudbank at the marsh as the wake washes where it had been quietly minnow stalking. And it flys into the lengthening shadows, squacking still, and across the wide marsh to get far away from this disturbance that has come so rudely into its world.

Johanna is standing among the docked trawlers on the dock as y'all slowly now approach. So you walk forward and toss her the bowline and she puts it over the piling. Then Forrest reverses Mustang and gets her stern coming in. So you walk back to toss Johanna the sternline. She sees from your faces how y'all did, so she doesn't even bother to ask. Then Forrest cuts the hard throbbing engine. And suddenly the silence is huge.

"I fixed a pot roast, Ben, come eat with us," she says. But you look at Forrest for permission. He only shrugs. So you say, "sounds great, Johanna, I'm starved." Then you see Carol standing among the parked cars and trucks beyond the dock and among the much darker now shadows of the live oaks with the Spanish moss hanging from them like old mens' shaggy and grey stained beards. So you wave. Then she waves. Then you remember how many times in recent weeks that you have seen Carol somewhere near but always in the background.

CHAPTER THREE

So you are bringing the supper dishes from the table where you all had eaten to the sink where Johanna is washing them and rinsing them and placing them in the rack to dry. Now you suddenly realize how impolite it is for you to keep going on and on in praise of all things North Carolina in comparison to Georgia. So you just as suddenly stop your rudely going on and on in comparison. But Johanna continues to smile weakly without comment with her head slightly bowed over the sink. So you know that you have hurt her feelings about her home here that she loves deeply just as you love your home deeply. And now your awkwardness becomes even more uncomfortable. Because Johanna has been especially nice to you since you have been down here. And the last thing that you would want to do is to hurt her feelings. But now you have hurt her feelings. So you quickly change the subject by asking her about Carol.

"Who, Carol Durant?" she looks up and says in welcoming the change of subject.

"Is that her last name? I see her a lot walking the dirt road to the dock. Early morning and late evening and other times just standing in the background at the dock. But she always waves to me and smiles. And we've talked briefly several times. But it sure is strange seeing such a pretty girl at such odd hours when you wouldn't expect to."

"Yeah, that's Carol Durant alright. I guess we are so use to seeing her, we really don't notice her. She stays with her Aunt in the brick house where you turn off the paved road onto the dirt road going to the dock. Several years ago her Dad and Brother had their trawler anchored for the night in Doboy Sound during a storm. They were rammed by a trawler making an illegal shrimp drag. Their trawler sank, and her Brother drowned. Her Dad's back was broken. He lives in Brunswick now. And he gets around fairly well now. Carol goes to take care of him sometimes. And I think she takes classes at Brunswick College. Her Mother disappeared when Carol was real young. Just disappeared. No one has seen or heard from her since." Then Johanna pauses and looks at you with the hurt feelings look now completely gone. "Why, you aren't interested in Carol, are you Ben?""Well, she is pretty. And she's strange enough to be interesting."

"Yes, she is pretty. But she's too young for you, Ben. And she is strange because her whole family is strange. Always has been. And not strange in a funny way. The men have always been shrimp thieves. Rather steal five dollars worth, than earn ten dollars worth. Bootleg oysters and clams during the off-season. Rob crabbers' pots. Whatever. If it's illegal, they were always mixed up in it. The ramming by another shrimp thief seemed like proper justice to us somehow. But Carol is alright, I guess. But you can do better, Ben. My best friend from high school works in Atlanta. She's coming home for the weekend. Maybe I'll get a chance to introduce you to her. Now she is pretty, and I mean really pretty."

But you have already decided that Carol is old enough and pretty enough and interesting enough. And now with the after supper clean up finished, you and Johanna are sitting on high stools at the kitchen bar. But weariness is quickly spreading through you, after the several beers with the big meal, and these after such a long and hot and futile day. And you feel a yawn rising, but you stop it in time. Then suddenly you wonder where Forrest has been so long.

"Where's Forrest?"

"In bed. He does this almost every night. Three ice tea glasses of whiskey and whatever, and a huge meal that three men couldn't eat. Then gone to bed without a word. No wonder he has gained so much weight."

"Oh, well then I better go. It's nine thirty now, and four o'clock will come real early."

"At least finish your beer, Ben. It's nice having someone to talk to."

And you do want to know more about what Forrest said about Mexico. And you can always get another hour of sleep on the way out in the morning.

"Johanna, was Forrest serious about our going to Mexico when the shrimp season ends here?"

"Sure, Ben. And he really does like you in spite of all the arguing that y'all do. He says that you are the best striker that he has ever had. But first we have to get a Mexican license. And there is a lot of politics involved in getting one. A business friend of ours in Miami is doing the mountain of paperwork for us. We made a great deal of money when we went there before. And I do mean a great deal of money. It will be like Forrest said, the bigger trawlers, the Sea Rover and the Capt. Sam will trawl continuously, and you will ferry Mustang to the dock several times a week to sell the shrimp and to bring back fuel and supplies. And everyone will make a great deal of money. If we can get the politics worked out first. And Forrest thinks that we can this year."

Then on the way to your house you can see Herb's car parked at the Laughing Gull. You haven't seen him for several weeks, and you have been wondering if things are going any better for him. But you really should go on and go to sleep. Because tomorrow will be another long and hot and futile day. But you cannot stop thinking about making five thousand dollars a week in Mexico for the several months of the off-season here. And Herb has been down here for several years. So he should know something about it.

Herb is from Southport, which is in southern coastal North Carolina and not very far from the South Carolina line. There it looks a lot like here, with hundreds of square miles of marsh cut by many creeks and rivers and bays. Except there is clear water and sandy bottom there, rather than the muddy water and boggy bottom that is here. Herb has shellfish leases here. He clams in spring and summer, and oysters in fall and winter. But he will do either or both whenever he has a buyer. And he is a very hard worker. And he can quickly tell you more than you ever wanted to know about oysters and clams. But it is really only a survival income for him. Because of the everywhere boggy mud bottom and the too big tides that are here, certainly, but also because of the much greater distance from here to the much more lucrative northern seafood markets. Herb's wife comes down to visit him from time to time. But she does not stay for very long at a time. Because she calls this place here, Bubbaville. And not laughingly.

There is Herb, there beyond the smoke and the pool table noise. There sitting on a stool and hunched over a beer. There glumly looking at himself in the mirror that is behind the bar. But first you must sidestep your way through the loitering about redneck crabbers and shrimpers who are doing more foul mouth arguing among themselves than pool shooting. And as usual, their trash talk ceases as you pass between them. But they only grudgingly make way with hostile looks and sullen stares, hoping upon hope to pushing you to the point of provocation to saying something anything. And in hearing their foulness, and in seeing their sullenness, you are hearing and seeing their fathers and their sons as well.

His glum face quickly brightens when he sees you come up behind him in the mirror. "Hey Ben!" And you all shake hands as you sit on the stool. "So how's shrimping?" he asks, clearly glad to see you.

"A handful a day, and there doesn't seem to be an end to it."

"Yeah, well, it's always something when you work the water."

"That's the truth for sure." Then the bartender brings a beer and you pay for it, as you settle on the stool. "So how's clamming?"

"Good news, bad news, as usual. Got thirty bags going to a new customer on Long Island this afternoon. He said he would reorder if he likes the quality. Oh, and a neighbor of yours is freighting them for me. Woodrow Fulcher and Sons in Sea level."

"Yeah, they've been freighting seafood for as long as I can remember. Good people usually. But sometimes they get a little too proud of their service."

"Yeah, that's the bad news. Their truck brought down crabbait fish, and it's picking up clams on the backhaul. They said two cents a clam for freight on the phone. But this afternoon they said four cents. I had to pay it, or get stuck with thirty bags of clams. They know that. Hell Ben, I'm only getting twelve cents a clam delivered. After digging them and grading them and bagging them and tagging them, and the cooler overhead and the wear and tear on my boat and motor, it's hardly worth the effort," and he sighs a thoroughly disgusted sigh. "But it's always something when you work the water, as I always say."

So you dry laugh and sadly shake your head again to that well-worn saying. "That's the truth for sure, Herb." Then you feel a suddenly sharp poke in your back. And you suddenly straighten and look around and see Jerry Harrelson pretending as though he had been making a pool shot and had accidentally poked you with the cue butt. But rather than apologize, he just stands there and

21

sullenly looks at you as a dare for you to say something anything. Then Herb firmly puts his hand on your arm.

"Let it go, Ben. Just let it go. You hit him, and we'll have to fight all these rednecks. They're assholes. They're worthless human beings. They aren't worth it. And especially Jerry."

So you try to get a hold to your suddenly flared temper. And you begin to unclinch your fist. Then you turn your hot hard look around and look at Jerry in the bar mirror. He sees your hot hard look in the mirror looking at him. But he only stands there smiling now. Then finally he turns and walks around the pool table.

"May as well kill the son of a bitch now and get it over with, Herb."

"He's too ignorant to care if you did. Just let it go, Ben."

"Now or later, Herb, it's only a matter of when."

"Then what? He isn't worth it. I beat him so bad when I first came here that he was in the hospital for three days. But did he learn anything? Hell no. And he never will. Look at his face. Those bruises are from Claudes' beating him several weeks ago. He's an ignorant redneck who will never learn. Just let it go. He isn't worth busting up your hands on while beating him senseless."

So you motion to the bartender for two beers. He brings them and you pay for them. And you are still trying to just let it go. Herb takes his hand from your arm. Then in another minute you have pretty well let it go.

"Herb, I have to go after this beer anyway. Have to get up at four to leave the dock at five. And I should already be asleep. But I wanted to stop and ask if you've heard anything about boats from here shrimping Mexican waters during the off season."

"What, is Forrest all fired up about that again?"

"I don't know about again. This is the first I've heard about it. At supper tonight he said that we would go in January and come back in April. And that I could make five thousand dollars a week. And Johanna agreed."

"Sure, you could have ten years ago, and probably would have. Most strikers did back then, Ben. And the boat owners a great deal more. That's when Forrest and Johanna went, the one and only time. And they probably made a ton of money. But soon after the Mexican Government wised up and began building their own shrimp fleet, rather than licensing foreign trawlers. Their waters hadn't been shrimped very much until then, so really big bucks were at stake. A few owners from the States still get licenses. But they have international pull. I mean really big time pull. Forrest and Johanna don't have that kind of pull. Sure, they own three trawlers and a shrimp dock here. And that's big time pull for here. But it's still only local pull, not international pull."

"Oh. I didn't know all that." And you can only sit there all mired in sudden disappointment. "But they said a friend of theirs in Miami is working on getting a license for them." As you grasp for any straw.

"Ben, he's only an agent. He works for anyone who pays him. Every year they send him his several thousand dollar fee. And every year he tells them how close they came, and maybe next year. Or at least that's what I've heard. But I could be wrong." As Herb sees your sudden disappointment, and is now trying to soften it.

"Well, it did sound too good to be true. But I sure hate that it is." Then you see in the bar mirror that most of the rednecks, Jerry included, have gone home to sleep, to do their whichever fishing tomorrow, then to be back here drunk and trash talking tomorrow night. So you begin to gather your change. But now the bartender brings the two beers that you didn't see Herb motion for. You start to protest. Then you shrug and think, hell I've gone fishing with too little sleep plenty of times before.

"Don't get me wrong, Ben, Forest and Johanna are damn fine people. Honest, hard working, and most years they make a good living from shrimp around here. Ten years ago they just happened to be in the right place at the right time, and got handed a pot of gold. But that was pure luck, and it won't happen again. But every year they hope it will."

"And I was hoping that they were about to hand me a pot of gold." Still feeling foolish.

"That's natural, Ben, we all do it. Hell, when I got this thirty thousand acre shellfish lease, I thought the Georgia DNR was handing me a pot of gold. And ten years before, it probably was. Just as Mexican shrimp no longer is the bonanza it was. Everything is overfished now, everywhere. That, or the market for that product is no longer there. Besides, Forrest has gotten too spooked by his ghost sailboat to ever venture far from here again.

Much less all the way to Mexico."

"Ghost sailboat?"

"Yeah. You haven't heard about that yet?"

"No. What ghost sailboat?"

"Swears that there is an abandoned silver and black sailboat with all sails set, that is stalking him and one day will run him down."

"That's the silliest thing I've ever hear, Herb."

"It has become real as hell to Forrest, though. You know that there have always been abandoned for whatever reason boats drifting around the oceans. More so now with all the drug smuggling. And especially this close to the Carribean. He has seen it three times in the past five years. Or so he says. Always at night when he is alone at the wheel, on trips north or south when he is looking shrimp. It appears out of nowhere, and slices close across his bow. Swears that it is stalking him, and one day will run him down. And it really does have him spooked, Ben."

"We fishermen are a superstitious bunch, but that's taking it too far. Forrest and I have argued several times about going to look for shrimp, and again this evening, but he just won't do it. I said it's because he wants to be home every night so he can pat Johanna on the ass."

"Well, that may be some of why he only shrimps around here." Herb says smiling. "After all, Johanna does have an ass that any man would like to pat every night. But it is his ghost sailboat too. It really does have him spooked."

But the weariness from this long day has begun to come in waves. But as your reach to gather your change and start to say that you are going, in the mirror you see the door open and two very good looking girls come in who are dressed much too well for a place like this. "Herb," you say as you nudge him and motion to the mirror.

"Yeah. The blonde is Georgia McIntosh. Don't know the other one. Probably a friend of hers."

"Serious? Georgia McIntosh in McIntosh County, Georgia?"

"Serious. She's from here. And that's her name. From a fishing family going way back. But she's too good for all that now. Does modeling in Atlanta. A redneck girl turned very high class."

And watching Georgia in the mirror, you say, Wow!, outloud. Because she has on pale tan boots of the softest leather you have ever seen. And sky blue jeans of the softest denim you have ever seen. And a sun yellow blouse of the softest cotton you have ever seen. With shimmering blonde hair that surrounds a face with the clearest skin you have ever seen. And turning on the stool to watch her, you say, Wow!, outloud again.

But Herb only shakes his head and laughs,"forget it, Ben. She's so far out of your league, you can't even see the ballpark. You'll just get your feelings hurt."

But you go anyway and put a quarter on the pool table rail where Georgia and her friend have started a game.

"What's that for?" she asks, in the huskiest voice you have ever hear.

"Winners," you say, but not as forcefully as you had intended.

"This is just a friendly game." she says, but you cannot see beyond the bright red of her lips.

"Rules say that anyone can play winners," someone says, and you think that it is you.

"Not this time," she says, and with a look so steady that it does not flinch.

So finally you say, "yes ma'am," and go get your quarter from the rail.

CHAPTER FOUR

So you have Mustang idling ready and the coffee made when Forrest comes onboard at five o'clock. And he says morning, and you say morning, as you pass each other in the wheelhouse. Then he settles into the big captains' chair before the controls, and you go and begin to cast off the lines.

Then you are dozing in your bunk while Forrest drives Mustang through the darker darkness that is right before dawn, out of the narrow Intercoastal Waterway and into the much wider Doboy Sound. But the heat and the humidity are already too high and too close around for so early. So the bunk sheets feel damp and they smell musty sweaty, and your shirt and jeans stick to you where you are lying on them. And there are already too high swells from the too strong southwest wind for so early also. So right away Mustang begins a harsh rolling and pitching that she rarely gets here inside. And somewhere inside your dozing you know that it is going to be a very rough all day out on a hard wind blown ocean where just holding on while you walk around the sterndeck will be difficult enough, much less your working in it amid unsteady nets and cables and trawl doors. But maybe this hard wind will scare some of the Sound shrimp, and they will rush out the Inlet with the falling tide where you and Forrest will be with Mustang.

And some do get scared out until by early afternoon you all

are working on your third one hundred pound box of big mid twenties count shrimp, which is one hell of a lot better than it has been that is for damn sure. Because your share is already close to two hundred dollars, and that is way more than you have made total for the past week of every days. So you are on your knees on the sterndeck and braced against the rolling and the pitching before the large pile of every sea creature that lives in these waters here close to the beaches. And you are culling the shrimp and the fish from the everything else swiftly and precisely and happily.

Then Forrest sticks his head out of the wheelhouse door and yells over the engine noise and the wind in the rigging noise. "Haul back, Ben! Now!!"

So you straighten up still on your knees and look over the rail the one hundred and eighty degrees from starboard to stern to port. But you do not see anything out of the ordinary. You all have been trawling back and forth on the north side of the long hooked shoal that leads to the south side of Doboy Inlet. In for the several miles on the side of the long shoal as the tide falls, haul back and turn, then out for the several miles of the long shoal that finally hooks toward the deep ocean. You do not see any trawlers inside of the shoal where the southwest wind has piled up a pounding surf onto the now exposed banks, and into the churning cuts and gullies and sloughs that are there. Several trawlers are trawling off shore of you all. But they are trawling ordinarily, so you wonder what the problem is.

"Now!! Godammit Ben!!"

So you are up quickly and at the winch, and start the two big trawl nets to coming in. Then you run around to the port side of the wheelhouse and look. And there off your bow as big as life itself, there is the Sea Warrior with her outriggers down and trawling and right before piling up onto that side of the long hooked shoal. With the hard southwest wind to her stern steadily pushing her along forcing her along to her doom want to or not rather not or not.

Then at the wheelhouse door you hear Forrest on the radio. "I warned you an hour ago that there was too much wind and not enough water inside that hook. Slicer, I warned you thirty minutes ago to haul back and get the hell out of there while you still could."

"Well, Cap, looks like you were right." Came back Slicers slow drawlily far away voice.

"Claude, you on?"

"Yeah, Forrest."

"Call St. Simon Coast Guard and tell them the Sea Warrior is going to pile up onto the shoal in about five minutes."

"Okay. Yeah, I see her. We're about hauled back now. Then will come to you."

"Okay, Claude. Slicer, you all better get off her before she hits."

"Well, Cap, we're still trying to get hauled back. Then we should be able to get her turned."

"Too late. You're already too shallow. You'll never get the trawls up. She'll start pounding to pieces as soon as she hits, Slicer."

"You reckon, Cap?" Came back his slow drawlily far away voice without a care in the world without a concern in the world.

So you go aft and get the nets and cables and doors dumped on the sterndeck to be straightened out later. A quick glance, and you see a good amount of shrimp thrashing about in the tailbog along with the everything else that is in there. Then you reset the outriggers down for better stability. Then you look and see Claude in the Princess several miles seaward and coming this way fast. As is another trawler seaward of her that you cannot make out the name of. But all any of you will be able to do is to get Slicer and Mike and Mikes' scruffy old bulldog Petey safely aboard one of your trawlers. Because there really isn't anything that anyone can do now to save the Sea Warrior. Because Forrest is right, Slicer doomed her first an hour ago, then again thirty minutes ago, when he didn't haul back and get turned out while he still could. So since then things have simply been going along step by step, minute by minute, to this obvious known end. The mistake now having compounded itself finally to this.

With Slicer probably so blown away on pot once again that it is as though he has a balcony seat to a sea adventure that is happening to someone else at a remote distance and in slow motion. But you look and you see that the destruction of a really fine trawler is real soon now. And with that fact now so clear it all suddenly becomes so real and so heartbreaking and so wasteful and so scarey. Because Sea Warrior is already in the surf of the shoals there inside the hook where spray and white water is being thrown up and up and out and out and everywhere. With her trawl cables tightly running aft and straining and now rising horizontally as they quickly now get shallower, and are holding Sea Warrior like sea anchors to going only straight ahead into the sharp inside curve of the hook there. With Slicer having hard righted the wheel minutes ago, so that Sea Warrior herself is now sluiced around to the right, but crab walking straight ahead death walk like anyway. Then you see Mike come out of the wheelhouse with a small canvas bag of his personal gear. And he sees you and he throws out both arms in a big shrug that says oh hell here we go and I sure as hell dread it. Then you see Petey on the sterndeck looking aft as though judging the situation. Then he is beside Mike with both front paws on the rail and looking out towards you. Then he looks at Mike with a look that says I'm with you pal, just say when. Petey, Mike's best buddy and constant companion and older now, and trawler raised and trawler wise, with the sagging jowls and the sad droopy eyes of all bulldogs.

Then you see Slicer stick his head out of the wheelhouse door with a totally unconcerned expression on his face, as though he is simply looking around and about outside to see whether it looks like rain. Then you are at your wheelhouse door, and you hear Forrest hollering outloud to himself as he is also pounding his hand on the wheel in full frustration.

"I told Sam Cox not to let Slicer Captain her. I told him that just last month. He asked me about Slicer, and I told him about Slicer. I told him that Slicer has already sunk two trawlers, and that

Sea Warrior will be the third trawler he'll sink. I told him that plain. I did tell him that plain. But did he listen? Hell no! Hell no he didn't listen. I told him that Slicer's nothing but a pot head. I did tell him that. Now look what Slicers' gone and done." So you go and gather several throw rings and several coils of line and several life preservers. And now you have these on the deck by the rail at the wheelhouse door. And now you can only helplessly watch as Sea Warriors' bow rises suddenly and sharply, and then slams down hard so hard there on the first shoal.

And it is like she has been slapped really hard by a giant hand that immediately stops her forward motion. So that both of her long outriggers slash forward then snap back then bend sharply and break in two loud cracks like two almost simultaneous rifle shots that the wind quickly brings to now suddenly stunned you. This while a mighty shiver starts at her keel and then rises through out her in a violent shaking like the giant hand has also hit the projector so that this wild picture momentarily blurs into five trawlers. This while Mike and Petey tumble forward there behind the rail in a sudden pitch and sprawl.

"Ben, don't go overboard. Once they go overboard and swim in, there's enough joining dry bars for them to walk over to us. Tie off several lines and throw them over and you can pull them up."

"Okay."

"Claude, they hit."

"Yeah, I saw it."

"Claude, I'm going to put our bow to the bank and give her enough throttle to keep us there, and let them walk to us."

"Okay. I'll ease to your stern and Johnny will jump over to help Ben get them up."

"Okay, Claude. Slicer? Slicer!?"

"Yeah, Cap."

"She's breaking up, Slicer. Y'all get off now. That's all y'all can do."

"You reckon, Cap?" Drawlily still totally unconcerned.

"You wormy goddam pothead, you've sunk another trawler! You're a worthless piece of shit, Slicer!"

"Now Forrest, there ain't no call to talk like that."

"Get off, Slicer! Now! There's nothing else y'all can do!"

"Well, if you think so, Cap."

Then over the radio with the crackle of the distance, Johanna comes on, and in a small voice says, "Forrest, y'all be careful."

"By God, I'm ashamed to be called a commercial fisherman the same as him! By God I am!" Forrest hollers outloud to himself as now he has the bow to the bank and then throttles up enough to keep it there. Then Johnny comes running around the wheelhouse from the stern just in time to see Sea Warrior rise for the second time, then slam down again in another so harsh pound that certainly begins the critical breaking of her vital ribs. "Jesus," Johnny says in whispered awe. And he looks at you and you look at him and you all look at Forrest and Forrest looks at you all. And

34

all of you all begin to sadly shake your heads in stunned disgust at the sheer waste and at the stupidity and at the danger of this whole sorry sad picture.

Then Mike and Petey are up again and at the rail. And they look as though they are trying to time their jump overboard right after a pound. But the pounds are coming too suddenly and too harshly and too close together now for them to get set and jump before they get knocked down again. Now they are knocked down behind the rail again. Then, amid these sudden pounds, it looks like the naval war movies you have seen of a destroyer shooting ashcan depth charges up and out in high lobbing tosses, as Mike with Petey in his arms as a single object are literally catapalted up and up and out and out in a high lobbing toss of their own. Then they hit the water in a big ball splash, and immediately both begin to separately swim to the nearest strip of dry sandbar that now and then is visible over there through the surf and the spray, in the wind and the noise.

Then, and just as suddenly, but almost as an after thought, Slicer is cartwheeled out of the wheelhouse door and out over the rail with his arms and his legs extended and distended like a flung away ragman doll, as though being thrown away in complete disgust in spewing vomiting even by the big hand. Then Sea Warrior's ribs simply cave. They simply cave. And now with each killing pound, she looks as though more and more air is being let out of her balloon. Until she simply settles as she deflates. Until now her keel and her bottom and her ribs are together with her sterndeck with no space in between. Then, all of the many upright boards of her wheelhouse outside wall simply come apart, simply fall apart, all fall down like pick-up sticks. And then they all begin to scatter and to drift in the wind and the surf and the noise and here and there and everywhere over there.

Then you are overboard and climbing up onto the sandbar that is under Mustangs' bow. And you have a throw ring in one hand and a coil of line in the other hand. And somewhere on the wind behind you hear Forrest holler, "Ben, don't!" But you could not simply stand by the rail and wait and watch and worry and wonder, and neither could he have. So now you are up on top of the bar and in the stinging blowing across sandy spray, and you quickly see the pattern of sloughs and dry bars that are in between you and Mike and Petey and Slicer.

Then you are to Mike and Petey. And you ask if they are okay and Mike says yeah I think and looks down and asks Petey if he is okay. But Petey only looks bulldog droopy sad eyed up at Mike as if to say yeah but some fine mess you got us in this time Ollie. Then Petey tries to shake off the water. But the hard wind blows another sheet of sandy spray and all of you are drenched again. Then you see Slicer coming toward you all. But he is trudging a straight line across the exposed bars then falling into the deep sloughs with a big splash. Then somehow getting across that slough and to the next bar and standing up only to get across it then fall splashing into the next slough as though in a particular daze of his very own.

So you all stand and wait for Slicer to stumble his way to you, your backs turned as much as possible to the loud blowing sandy spray. Then in a rush of words, as though he just remembered, Mike says he knew better, he really did. That he had sworn to himself never ever to get on a boat with Slicer. But that Slicer had stopped by last night begging him to come with him today just this once, that his regular striker was in jail for brawling and public drunk and he needed to make today so he could make the bail money. And Mike says his boat is tied to the dock waiting for clutch parts, so in that moment he suddenly really did feel sorry for Slicer. So he came today just this once to help him out of a bind. Then Mike can only stand and shake his head in I don't know how I could have been so stupid bewilderment. And spit sandy sea water and wipe it from his eyes also, as you all continue to watch Slicer stumble tumble the last distance to here. Then Mike finishes his word rush by saying, "I knew better, I really did Ben."

Slicer is close enough now for you to see the particular dazed look of his very own. And you see that he had hit a sandbar on his nose and forehead when the giant hand threw him from Sea Warrior in a cartwheel vomit away in total disgust. So the skin is deeply scrapped there, and blood is running down his face and mixing with the sandy sea-water and his spit. And then Slicer nonchalantly walks right up to you and he asks, "hey Cap, got a beer?"

The stern faced Coast Guardsmen in orange jumpsuits and with forty fives on their hips are definitely not in a hey how are you I am fine how are you mood, for sure. They tied off their cruiser outside of Mustang several minutes ago as soon as Forrest finished docking. And Slicer and Mike with Petey are already on board the cruiser. And the no bullshit serious investigation is already underway. And Slicers' particular dazed look looks in definite need of a booster now that it has begun to wilt. And Mike looks like he is looking for a magic trap door through which he and Petey can simply drop through and disappear completely with none of this mess really happening. With Petey looking up at Mike as if saying, well, are you happy now Ollie? And with the on looker crowd on the dock and spreading beyond still growing by the minute. After all, this is real excitement where very little excitement ever happens.

Now Johanna comes on board Mustang and gives Forrest a hug. Then she comes smiling to you and gives you a big hug also, and says, "gosh, I'm so proud of you two guys." So right away you begin to swell up like some kind of hero real or not doesn't matter. But over Johanna's shoulder you see so very sophisticated Georgia McIntosh with her hands on her hips and standing on the dock and looking over this sea rescue aftermath dramatic scene with so cool disinterest and such sophistication. But beyond Georgia, at the parked cars and trucks and at the edge of the still growing crowd, you see that Carol is waving big to you and that she is just beaming her pride of you.

CHAPTER FIVE

But the next day the wind goes east and a little south. And it lays to only now and then puffy breezes as though it no longer is interested. As though the glaring heat has stifled the wind also. So the shrimp that had been stirred up and scared out by the hard southwest wind now remain idling in billowing schools that constantly shift and drift all along the winding creeks and the winding rivers. And gradually these bellows settle, shifting and drifting still, further down the water column and away from the stifling heat at the glaring surface.

But you all go trawling for the next several days anyway. Out of still being in the rut of if you don't go, you don't know. Out of being in the rut of since you feel you should go today, then you may as well go tomorrow. And since you go tomorrow, you may as well go the following day. Out of the stubbornness and the hardheadedness of believing that persistence always pays. But it doesn't always, and it doesn't usually, and it doesn't during these days either. So finally Forrest says that the next day you all will haul Mustang out onto the rail for the two days that it will take to scrape and to clean and to paint her bottom to get that hardwork dirty chore done and over with until winter at least. And that suits the hell out of you.

And for lunch the first day Johanna brings thick sliced roast beef sandwiches and potato salad and pickles and iced beer. So right away you and Forrest go to the hose to wash off the dead red bottom paint and the dried green slime from your faces and hands. Then the three of you sit close together on overturned five gallon buckets to eat and to talk small talk and to enjoy the big shade cool of Mustang looming high overhead. And when there is a pause in the eating and the small talking, you quietly ask Johanna whether Georgia is still down. But Johanna quickly says no, that she has already gone back to Atlanta. But you still want to ask Johanna what happened to her bringing you all together maybe at a party at their house. But clearly now Johanna does not want to talk about Georgia anymore. So right away you know that she did ask she did try. But that Georgia had said no, hell no, why on earth would I want to spend any time with a scroungy damn shrimper. So now Johanna does not want to hurt your feelings by saying that. So you change the subject as gently as you can. But you have already felt the hurt in hurt feelings.

Then to fill this awkward silence Johanna quickly says that she heard at the grocery store earlier that the Coast Guard is going to throw the book at Slicer, including a twenty-five thousand dollar fine for the fuel spill as well as a charge for boating while under the influence. But right away Forrest grumbles, hell, they said that at his other sinkings too but nothing ever came of it. But soothingly Johanna follows by saying, well, maybe they really will put a stop to him this time, someone sure needs to. But somehow she does not say this with a great deal of certainty. And Forrest shakes his head and says, well, I sure hope the hell they do this time because he makes me ashamed to be a commercial fisherman. And you wholeheartedly nod your agreement to this but without it really getting too much into what has clearly now become their conversation about one of their own people here. Then Forrest goes on to say, but everyone here in this county is kin to everyone else here by marriage if not by blood, so getting a jury conviction for anything serious is damn near impossible because any jury will have a least several kin on it, and whatever else kin do do here they do stick together. Because they may cut each other or stomp each other or kill each other but they will never not ever convict each other, so that son of a bitch Slicer will probably walk again this time to boat sink again. But you wisely just keep your mouth shut because suddenly now you understand that this is a local problem and if the locals cannot solve it then an outsider sure as hell cannot solve it so it is best to just keep your mouth shut or else they will turn on you for butting into what is obviously none of your business. But again suddenly you now do better understand why McInctosh County is known far and wide as the criminal fisherman capital of Georgia if not the entire East Coast with the Gulf Coast thrown in for good measure yessir bubba bubba boy.

Then the next night Forrest phones to say that now that Mustang is fresh scraped and fresh painted and back overboard he and Johanna have decided to go inland to visit friends and to just get away from trawlers and from shrimp fishing for a couple of days at least. But that he had talked with Claude and Claude had said that you can double up with Johnny striking on Princess for these couple of days just to keep some little bit of money coming in if you want to. But right away you begin to hem and haw and to otherwise stall while you think fast because right away the thought of getting completely away from trawlers and from shrimp fishing for a couple of days sounds mighty good to you also. So you tell Forrest that you aren't sure that you'll think about it that you may just get away from it all for these couple of days also. And he says for you to suit yourself. But that Claude had said that you're welcome to double with Johnny if you want to. So you say okay thanks that you'll decide and let Claude know. And Forrest says fine, see you in a couple of days. And you say, yeah, y'all have a fun trip. And he says, yeah, we'll try.

So at the frig and with a new beer pressed cold to your too sunburned hot forehead you think that it would be great to clam with Herb for these couple of days, that is if Herb needs you which he probably doesn't but just maybe he does. So right away you phone Herb and right away Herb says hell yes he sure does need you. That the Long Island buyer had phoned this afternoon to say that he needs all the clams he can get for a big Seafood Festival weekend this weekend, but clamming alone Herb says he just can't get enough bags on such short notice to make the minimum number of bags of clams that Woodrow Fulcher and Sons needs to make it worthwhile to haul them that far. But clamming together we could no problem. Then Herb says, but Ben with freight costs and lease costs and everything, I can only pay you six cents a clam, but there's plenty of clams where we'll work so you should be able to get a thousand a day at least no sweat, which will be sixty dollars a day. And right away you say, fine, that that's a hell of a lot more money than you've been making a day here lately. So Herb says, great! that low tide is at noon so meet him at the dock a little before nine o'clock and you all will go in his skiff and work from it. So you say, great, sounds good Herb!

Because clamming these couple of days with Herb will be just the get completely away from it all kind of change that you need. Because being out on the water in a work skiff has a solitude and a satisfaction and a majesty all of it's own. There away from the loud drone and the jarring vibration of the trawlers diesel engine endlessly pounding along powerfully. There away from the clattering bangs of the winch and the twisting tangles of the nets and the cables and the trawl doors. There away from having to again and again and once again cull through the piles and the piles of literally everything that lives in the along the beaches ocean, that is tailbag dumped on the sterndeck after each trawl every hour or so all day long day after day week after week.

So right away you remember the many times that you have oystered or clammed alone or with your brother Tommy from a work skiff the length and the width of Core Sound there back home and the peaceful sense of accomplishment that bay fishermen have that no other commercial fishermen have. But now so fully remembering the sights and the sounds and the smells of Core Sound from a work skiff only brings the homesickness back, and really strong this time again. So you say to yourself whoa fella don't think about all that now. Because it will not help. Because it will only hurt. So you say to yourself hey fella for the next couple of days you and Herb will clam together from a work skiff, and that will be damn fun and a good change. And that is all you need to think about right now.

But the clams in Georgia are only in the shelly places in the feeder creeks that cut winding and winding far into the many marsh islands that are here and there and everywhere around and to the horizon and beyond, here behind the barrier islands that so bravely face the ocean sea. And bogging these black mud creeks for a hundred yards up a creek, then crossing through the thick marsh grass itself to the next creek, then bogging your way for a hundred yards back out, while hunched over and moving along quickly and looking for the clams that are in patches large or small or veins wide or narrow, is nothing but hot and hard and stinking and sweaty work work. But what a good change this clam fishing is from shrimp fishing. Because all commercial fishing is just bust ass work one way or the other anyway. And it is all you have ever done, and it is all you ever want to do.

But you can only clam in Georgia during low tide. Because in the narrow winding creeks the clam populations are too scattered to search for them with long handle tools from work shiffs during high tide. So your clamming workday is only four to five hours long. Which is another good change from your shrimping workday of from can't see to can't see long. But while the workday length is much shorter, the work effort expended is much more concentrated. So the bust ass total is the same, only the intensity level changes. But you average eighty dollars a day for these couple of days in spite of being out of practice for fast clam harvesting and out of shape for speedily bogging mud creeks. And this is much needed money and therefore so very welcome. And with low tide during the middle of the day, you can sleep late and still have time for breakfast and getting ready before meeting Herb at the dock. And you all are through clamming and in by three or four in the afternoon, which is nice for coming here to the Laughing Gull for several beers and a game of pool and some fisherman talk before the rednecks have a chance to school up and to bring the dark cloud trouble that follows them everywhere to this now quiet place.

"They promised me the moon to come down here and turn those rundown leases into something successful. Grants, technical assistance, low cost loans, you name it, whatever they thought it would take to get me here. Remember that they are marine biologists and bureaucrats, and that they have never dug a clam or picked an oyster commercially in their lives. And that other than bootlegging oysters and clams during the off season, the fishermen here either crab or shrimp. They are not shellfish fishermen. So no one knew whether the resources were commercially viable. But once I was here and committed and with my bridges mostly burned back to North Carolina, all of their promises just disappeared like smoke three months later. They just cut me loose to sink or swim on my own, root hog or die. Then they wouldn't even return my increasingly frantic phone calls. What happened? I don't know. Maybe the Atlanta bureaucrats decided that the Brunswick bureaucrats were getting too big for their britches, and pulled the rug out form under them.   Since shrimp is king here, and has the political clout, maybe the shrimper decided they didn't want a new fishery competing with them. I don't know. And I'll probably never know. But with some support and some seed money, we could have developed one hell of a shellfish resource. Especially oysters, with oysters there is no limit down here. But one broke assed shellfish fisherman cannot do it alone no matter how hard he tries or how much he cares. So---." Herb says trailing off. Then he sadly shakes his head in the mirror behind the bar, his lips pursed and his teeth clinched.

"So what are you going to do?" You say turned on the stool with an elbow resting on the bar and looking at him with concern. But Herb already shows the damage in his face and hands of too many hot summers and too many cold winters working the water. As do all commercial fishermen, you included.

Then with increasing bitterness Herb says. "Ben, I've never failed at anything before in my life. Sure, there have been times when things haven't worked out as well as I had hoped they would. But no total failures. Not like this failure. Not five years and thirty thousand dollars, gone. Just gone. Bobby Ann keeps saying for me to cut my losses and come home. To pack up and just walk away from all the debt and investment as a lost cause. She says, why should a North Carolinian care more for Georgia shellfish than Georgians do? And she's right, Ben. But somewhere along the way my pride got involved. So maybe my judgement really is clouded. But, Ben, the potential for oysters here is huge, it really is. But so are the problems. They are just too huge for one man to solve alone. And I realize that. But I also realize that admitting failure, finally, is still too bitter for me to do. I just can't do that yet. Because building an oyster industry here is a win win situation for everyone. There are no down sides, Ben. The resource wins, the ecology wins, the water quality wins, jobs win, taxes wins, the State wins, everyone here wins. Why can't anyone else see that?" And now Herbs' eyes show the sad damage that comes from too close exposure to bureaucrats with their own political agenda. "So I'm clinging to that old one last hope that maybe things will get better. So I'm going to give it one more oyster season, this fall and winter. If it's a good season, with really good sales, then there's still hope. Maybe I still can turn things around."

And in hearing Herb, you realize again just how very much most commercial fishermen of whichever fishery really do care about what they do and where they do it. So you say, "Herb, I'll be on the boat most of the time until the shrimp slow in December. But anything I can do to help, you know I'll be glad to."

"Thanks Ben, I appreciate that. Just having someone to talk to who isn't a Georgia redneck is a big help." And Herb smiles. But he really means it. "Also, I'm thinking about buying a used refrigerated truck so I can deliver the oysters over a larger area.

47

But that will mean putting another five or six thousand dollars of borrowed money into the business, which is probably throwing more good money after bad. Once again, my heart says do, but my head says don't. If I do, you can help me get the oysters picked and delivered when you're not on the boat. That is if you want to."

"Sure Herb, be glad to. Just let me know."

Then Herb is silent. But you can almost hear the rumbling argument between his heart and his head. But with his total failure already all but a certainty, you hope that this time he listens to his head. Because the obstacles he faces are too great and there are too many of them. But then each of us have to make our own decisions whether want to or not, then live with the consequences of those decisions whether good or bad. And as the silence between you all continues you hope upon hope that this coming oyster season is a really good one for Herbs' sake. Because he has tried so hard, and because he cares so deeply. But in commercial fishing, as in everything else, nothing is ever easy, and only rarely do things turn out well, and if it can go wrong it usually does.

Then the door opens and right away the late afternoon sun and heat flood the cool dimness that is inside here. Then Mike and Petey are silhouetted in this hot glare. Then Mike closes the door. But for a minute you all have to adjust to this new dimness. Then you all see that Mike has drawn a wide circle around Peteys' left eye with a black marking pencil, and that it looks exactly like a bullseye. So right away you and Herb laugh outloud.

"What's Petey all duded up for, Mike?" you say still laughing.

"He's going courting, Ben. Aren't you, Petey? Isn't he one sharp dude, fellas?" and Mike looks down with full pride and love at his constant companion. Then he says, "Dan Lane's all brown female bulldog is in heat, and we're mating them. With Petey all white, we should get some real cute brown spotted puppies. Since they'll be full blooded maybe we can sell them and make some money."

So right away you and Herb begin to tease Petey about his up coming date. And right away Petey wags his stump tail to show that he understands. And this wag begins at his shoulders and goes back quickly until it finally involves his whole body, big droopy skin head included. "Look Ben, I saw your truck outside when I was going by. And I wanted to come in and explain why I was on Sea Warrior with Slicer."

"You've already explained, Mike, and I understand."

"Well, still, I'm going around to all the fellas to make sure you all understand that he was in a bind, and that I was just helping him out just that once. I damn sure don't want you all to think that I've started running with the likes of Slicer. And when Forrest gets back tomorrow, I'll go explain to him too."

But Mike had already explained to Forrest, as he had to you as well as all the fellas. But still he felt the need to explain again, and again. Then finally he quite formally shakes hands with you and with Herb, then and just as formally he and Petey leave for

Peteys' date.

"I don't blame Mike for being worried." Herb says to you in the bar mirror in the now once again cool dimness. "Shrimpers will overlook a fella slipping inside the closed waters line to take on illegal drag now and then when it is absolutely necessary. But get the name of boat sinker, or of running with a boat sinker, and they will gang up on you fast. That's true of shrimpers everywhere. And it's true that if a shrimper can't help you, at least he won't hurt you. But these shrimpers here will hurt you even when they can't help you, especially then. Out of spite, out of jealousy, out of ignorantly thinking that if I'm too worthless to succeed, at least I can stop you from succeeding. They have certainly hurt me even though my shellfish fishery doesn't have anything to do with their shrimp fishery. Mike knows how these fellas here are. And that is why he is so worried. And you should start worrying too, Ben. You're such a hard worker that you single-handedly work the sterndeck of Mustang. But it takes two of these fellas here to work the sterndecks of their boats, and they only half ass do that. That is what is behind Jerry Harrelsons' trying to provoke you. You, an outsider, are making them look bad. And they'll sneak around until they find a way to hurt you, Ben, really hurt you."

Then Herb looks grim faced from experience at you in the bar mirror. "Ben, you're in McIntosh County, Georgia, now. A world apart from the other world. And it is a bog, just as the clam creeks that we have been working are bogs. And it will stifle you and smother you and drag you down just as the creeks will. Just

50

remember that, Ben."

But the dog days have not ended. So the repetition continues. More long days with only a handful of shrimp at the end of them to show for the hard hard effort expended. But if you don't go, you don't know. And if you aren't there for the bad days, you will not be there for the good days. And perseverance pays. At least sometimes it pays. And hopefully it will pay this time. So you set your jaw, and do the days. Just set your jaw and do the days. Because nothing lasts forever. Because these days, too, shall end. Because the fall cool down, the fall shrimp run, is closer now. Much closer now. So close now that you can almost taste it. So close now that you can almost feel and hear the jingle of the coins of it in your pocket.

So you and Forrest go through your separate hard work routines quickly, efficiently, and without talking. After all, you each are very skilled very experienced at what you each do. So talking is not necessary. Words are not necessary. Only the routine is necessary. The routine and the chaos of the setting of the nets and the trawling of the nets and the hauling back of the nets and the dumping of the nets and the setting of the nets once again once again. Through the routine of the cleaning of the nets and the mending of the nets and the maintenance of the winch and the maintenance of the engine and the maintenance of the cables and the lines and the doors and the try net. Through the routine of the meals fixed in the galley and the cleaning of the galley and the changing of the bunk sheets. Through the routine of once again going to Foodland for more food and more supplies. Through the routine of once again taking on more ice and more fuel. With set jaw, with few spoken words, persevering through the all and the everything that is in living half of your life aboard a work boat, a commercial fishing workboat. But perfectly happy never the less, even in this endless unhappiness of a handful of shrimp, a handful of shrimp. Because this is all you have ever done. Because this is all you ever want to do.

And always there is the great beauty that is in each morning here in this hard toil world of yours as Mustang comes ghostlike out of Doboy Sound and through the Inlet in the darker darks that are always before the dawn that slowly now become the everywhere grey that now quickly become the many greys that now and again quickly become the many many yellows and pinks and blues, in vast streaks and splashes and flung shades and hues, until finally the gold sun suddenly now rises stark and round and enlarged from the far ocean over there and begins its bold climb.

And with the sun rise there is the wind rise also. As yet another work day aboard a work boat begins with the now continual motion of everything and everyone rolling and pitching and yawing that is within the continual noise of the wind passing and the swells rushing and the lines slapping and the cables twanging and the wood doors thudding and the winch grinding and the engine throbbing. As Forrest now has Mustang trawling along Sapelo Island beach in only fifteen feet of water so that the top of the beach side net is almost breaking the water and the water that it pushes rushes high up onto the beach as you go along the beach as a man made surf that for these moments is mightier than the natural surf as the flocking shorebirds scamper frantically to follow this much larger surf to capture the thrust out and now exposed sea life that is suddenly now washed up in it sprawling and thrashing for life and breath itself. But now with the jutting sandbars of Sapelo Inlet just ahead, Forrest begins a slow turnout. So you begin the hauling back of the nets. And the beach that for almost an hour you almost could have jumped from the rail onto gradually now begins to move away as the sandy beach with the sandy dunes beyond and with the highlands beyond them gradually now becomes more distant and therefore more distorted there behind the hot summer day haze. So, yes, this is all that you have ever done. So, yes, this is all that you ever want to do. And who in the world could ever blame you?

There is Carol. There once again walking the narrow dirt road that goes through the thick woods to the dock. With the evening sun slanted through the live oaks and the Spanish moss and the heat all around her like a light and shadow background. Then she steps to the side of the road and waves and smiles as you slow the truck to a stop.

"Hello, Carol."

"Well hello, Ben." As she comes still smiling to beside the truck.

"Haven't seen you lately. And I've been wondering where you were."

"You've missed me! Have you really missed me, Ben?" As her smile quickly goes from a greeting smile to a surprised smile to a pleasure smile.

"Well sure, Carol." But you begin to blush at how quickly she makes it very personal. "You always wave and smile and speak. The people around here aren't usually that friendly."

"Yeah, they can be pretty grim all right. Especially to outsiders. Just overlook them, they don't know any better. It's their redneck heritage." Then she shrugs. "I've just been taking care of my Dad in Brunswick. My Sister and I take turns. Nothing really mysterious."

"Yeah, Johanna said he was badly hurt in a trawler accident several years ago."

"Yeah, five years ago. My Brother was killed and Dad hurt his back and couldn't walk for awhile."

"I'm sorry." But you don't want to say that Johanna also said that her Dad and Brother weren't anything but shrimp thieves and always had been and probably got what they deserved. And that she hoped all shrimp thieves got run off the water one way or the other it didn't matter it serves them right.

"Well, you're a fisherman, you know how dangerous it can be." But when her smile went, it took with it most of her cuteness also. "Besides, Dads' much better now. He gets around okay, and could Captain again. But he says everything is different now, and he doesn't want to mess with it anymore."

"Well, there haven't been enough shrimp recently for it to be worth messing with anyway." But now you are uncomfortable with the subject of the conversation. Because with the overfishing of way too many legal trawlers already, the crackdown on shrimp thieves has become day and night relentless. And as a known shrimp thief, her Dad would be continuously watched, continuously harassed everytime he left a dock in a trawler. So, to change the subject from all that, you just blurt out, "look , Carol, I've got a big flounder we just caught, and I'm going to fix it for supper. And if you aren't doing anything maybe you can come over, or go with me now, or I can come pick you up, or something." And you are as surprised as Carol by the sudden rush of all this. And you lamely follow it with, "that is if you aren't doing anything, that is if you like flounder, that is if you want to.", and now the blush is back and it is quickly spreading and deepening.

"How could I be from a fishing family and not like flounder? All seafood in fact?" as her cuteness fully returns with her pure pleasure smile. "I would love to, Ben. I had started to worry that you would never ask me out, or over, or anything ever. And here I've been wearing this obvious sign, 'Hey, Ben, here I am,' all these months for you and everyone else to see." and now her smile is really big and she laughs easily. And her nose and her eyes get all crinkled up in the smile also. And she is really cute now, she really is.

"Well, I'm new here, and I didn't know, and I'm shy away from boats, and I wasn't sure. And everything", and now you feel past awkward and into ridiculous.

"Sure, Ben, I would love to. What time? ", as Carol doesn't make it any harder for you than it already is. As the first of the evening sea breeze gently moves among the live oaks and the Spanish moss and the heat, and the wave of wispy brown hair on Carols' forehead.

"It's seven now. Eight or eight thirty? If that's okay? I'll come get you."

"No, I'll drive over. What can I bring?"

"I have everything. Cabbage for slaw, cornmeal for cornbread, fries, the flounder of course. Unless you rather have something else?"

"No, that sounds fine, sounds good. I baked a cake this morning for my Aunt. I'll bring some of it."

"Okay, great. Sure I can't come get you? Do you know where I live?"

"No, I'll drive over. Yeah, Alex Wards' old house in Sapelo Gardens."

"Yeah. So okay, Carol, till later then", and now you are grinning.

"Till later, Ben.", and her smile is still crinkily.

So you see her in the rearview mirror. Then she turns and once again begins to walk the dirt road to the dock.

"Well, what the hell do you know about that?!" You say with a laugh as you drive along.

The evening seabreeze continues to move the heavy heat from here to there and back again, outside in the yard where the live oak limbs are so twisted and the Spanish moss is so sagging. But inside the house the big window air conditioner has the air cool and crisp and delicious. Now you and Carol are sitting on the couch. Carol is sitting cross-legged facing you. You are sitting with you feet on the floor and leaning forward and shuffling through the commercial fishing industry magazines that are scattered in piles about the coffee table. But each time you pick up a magazine and begin to thumb through it to find an interesting article to show to Carol, she takes the magazine from you and tosses it back with the other magazines.

"I said we aren't talking about fishing tonight, Ben."

"But the guys in Louisiana are trying out a new type of fish excluder in their trawls. It's interesting, let me show it to you." And you reach for the magazine. But she playfully slaps your hand down.

"I don't care what the guys in Louisiana are trying, silly. It doesn't have anything to do with you and me here and now.

"Then I don't know what to talk about." And you begin to fidget awkwardly. Because having spent more than half of you life on boats on the sea with only men and gear and machinery and weather as constant companions, you really cannot have conversations that do not include these. And conversations with women have always been especially awkward for you.

"You, me, us, anything. Anything that doesn't have to do with fishing." And Carols' crinkley smile around her nose and eyes has not left her face all during supper and then you all doing the dishes together and putting away the leftovers, or now that you all are settled here on the couch. "There is a world away from fishing, Ben, there really is."

"Of course there is, Carol, I know that. But."

"But fishing is all you know. I know, I've heard that and heard that, until I'll scream if I hear that again. Bores, fishermen are such bores. But never boring. Still, you have to have interests away from fishing, Ben. Watch."

Then she gets a pad and pencil from the coffee table. Then she holds the pad in front of herself so you cannot see it. Then she makes a quick series of sure strokes with the pencil. Then, and in only several seconds, she turns the pad for you to see.

"Seagull!" You say in complete surprise. "How did you do that?! " Because in only ten strokes or more, she has sketched what is clearly a seagull. Then she flips the page and again turns the pad so you cannot see it.

"Black skimmer!"

"Heron!"

"Marsh hen!"

"Oyster catcher!"

Then Carol tosses the pad and pencil onto the coffee table. Then she spreads her hands and says, "da, da," as though presenting herself. And now her crinkley smile is full of self pride also.

"Shore birds, Ben. You see them everyday. But you never really notice them. There's much more to out there than the endless fishing, fishing, fishing. Have other interests from it, Ben."

"Well, I'm, pretty good at whittling things. But you're really talented."

"It's a lot of practice. But mainly it's just really wanting to learn to. Make yourself learn to carve shore birds or boats or scrimsaw. The tourists love anything coastal. After I've checked on Dad, I go over to St. Simons Island and sit on a bench at the pier where the tourist gather. And I sell my shore birds as fast as I can sketch them."

"That's amazing, Carol. I didn't know you did that. You have always seemed mysterious the way you suddenly appear, then just as suddenly disappear."

"Independent, not mysterious. Being dependent on fishing killed my Brother and crippled my Dad, and wore my Mom out until she finally just left us. I swore never to be dependent of fishing. Or any fishermen. Not even you, Ben." Now her eyes begin to glisten through her crinkley smile. "When we're married, I will be independent of you, Benjamin Farrow Meekins. And you may as well know this from the first."

"Married!? We're getting married?!"

"Of course. Maybe not soon. But one day we will. I knew it for sure the day you and Forrest brought Slicer and Mike and Petey from Sea Warrior. You saw the look on my face. I saw you see it. And your smile and wave to me said, yes, that you knew it for sure too."

Then later Carol asks from the bedroom where the clean

sheets are. Then you hear her making the bed. And you stand at the frig and roll the just opened cold beer along the burnt black and painful sunburn on your forehead. And hearing her moving around back there as though she were at home, you realize how very lonely you have been. And that this has been a large part of the homesickness also.

And in the dimness of the hall nightlight, Carol comes to you under the sheet and says," so kiss me goodnight with our very first kiss." And the kiss is long that begins so tentatively. The long kiss that soon relaxes and softens as it lengthens until it finally becomes urgent.

And when your mouth begins to work the nipple of her breast, Carol says, "ooh." And when your hand begins to work between her legs, Carol says, "ooh!" And when your hard begins to work all the way inside of her, Carol says, "ooh, Ben, ooh!"

CHAPTER SIX

So finally all these weeks of days of a handful of shrimp, a handful of shrimp must have gotten deeply enough into Forrests' pocket for him to decide to go elsewhere to look for shrimp, ghost sailboat, or no ghost sailboat, and maybe I am just imagining that it is out there waiting to run me down anyway. Or more likely, he had a one sided conversation with his banker, and his banker made the decision for him. Because bankers have a ruthless way of getting right to the heart of a problem and suddenly shuffling your so long rigid priorities, whether you want for them to or not, whether you like the new shuffle or not, doesn't really matter. Yes hell they do too.

Because when Forrest just came aboard and you all are stirring sugar into your coffee standing sleepy eyed in the galley he says, "all right, so okay, look, Ben, we're going to South Carolina to shrimp for awhile. We'll try along the beach off St. Catherine's today. Then tomorrow we'll give Mustang a good maintenance and fix it going over.

Then we'll fuel and ice, and leave out. Okay?"

"It was okay with me a month ago."

"No smart ass, all right? Just letting you know."

"Right, Cap, aye aye Sir!," you say while saluting briskly. But for the next moment Forrest just stands there and shakes his head in the hopelessness of your endless smart assness. Then finally able to just ignore it, he says, "a friend of mine, David Sorensen, has a dock and several trawlers at Edisto Island south of Charleston. On the phone last night he said they're making decent paychecks, but nothing spectacular, and for us to come on up. Those boys don't need us up there getting their shrimp, but in the past they've come down here when the situations were reversed. So this is just returning the favor. We'll run all night, getting cat naps of sleep while we do, then be ready to start fishing at dawn. David said St. Helena Sound has been dependable for him the past few weeks. So we'll meet him there, and try there the first day, and see how it goes. Okay?"

And by now you have already set aside your smart assness. And you cannot keep back the silly looking toothy grin that has broken through what seemingly had become your permanent gloom and despair. Because suddenly now things do not seem so bad after all, like a roller coaster ride quickly going from darkness into light. Because shrimping South Carolina waters may not turn out to be any better than shrimping here. But then again maybe it will turn out to be better much better. And in going there, there is at least the hope of that. Where shrimping these waters here, at least until the fall cool down run, there is no hope. And hope and a good boat is all a commercial fisherman ever really wants.

Because commercial fishing is by far the most dangerous of all professions. So commercial fishermen naturally lean towards pessimism and fatalism. And commercial fishing is by far the most trial and failure oriented of all professions. So commercial fishermen must persevere doggedly determinedly and hunkered down through all of this endless trial and failure adversity. But only rarely do commercial fishermen handle sudden prosperity well. Whether a shrimper who stumbles on a swarming school of big shrimp. Or a clammer who happens upon a brimming hole of gorgeous littlenecks. Or a scolloper who chance drags across a cove size bed of palm size scollops. It is the sheer luck of finding them at all. It is the skill and experience it takes to harvest them. It is the absolute thrill of loading the boat with more of whichever resource than you have ever seen at one place at one time. That feat simply must be told and shared and bragged about. It simply must, and prosperity be damned. Because after all and everything what really counts is the recognition by your fellow fishermen that for a day, for several days even, you, yes you, are a true highliner top fisherman for that time however long or short. But in the telling and sharing and bragging about, you automatically shift the harvest money that would have gone into your pocket into another fishermans' pocket. And while you so briefly bask in the fast fading limelight, you swear to yourself that next time, if there is a next time, you will not tell or share or brag. But deep inside you know damn well that you will. Because that, too, comes naturally to commercial fishermen along with everything else.

And you still had the silly looking toothy grin when you got home last night. But Carol was not there to see it. And you had wanted so for Carol to see it after these past weeks of your moody grimness and your forever smart assness. But she probably went to Brunswick to visit her Dad and to sell her sketches at the pier on St. Simons for several days. So this morning you left her a happy note about you all going to shrimp South Carolina. And you can just picture the cute smile that she will have when she reads it. The same cute smile that you now so look forward to coming home to. But you do not know why she picked you from the many. But you are very glad that she did. As you both right away accepted the fact that for this time you all would live together. And now you do not want anything to disturb this so welcome change from the loneliness and the homesickness of before Carol. So you promise yourself that when you get back from South Carolina you will make certain that she continues to look forward to your coming home and even more so than before. And what would help that the most would be for you to bring back a really good paycheck from South Carolina. Because you have always been too competitive a fisherman to handle poverty with a shrug and a grin and bear it. But even if South Carolina is a bust, you promise yourself that in the future you will be a happier Ben for Carol.

It is late afternoon and into early evening before you all have Mustang pulling away from the dock. Her big diesel engine having only just begun its long haul endless work of day into night into day again work. Johanna there waving and smiling brightly. You waving back and smiling also. Even Forrest cannot keep back a smile. The good excitement of any voyage having infected all of you.

Now you all are running slowly along the Mud River channel that goes so near to the lefthand bank before long curving around and ending far to the right and at Sapelo Sound there so close to Sapelo Inlet and then the sea. This long curve being necessary to skirt the thousand acre mudflat that is Herbs' prime oyster beds. And in the slanting evening sun from this distance the oyster beds are black brown thick lines and shadowy bulges and glinting mounds that are contrasted to and raised above the sprawling dull brown brown mudflat. And there is Herb! There almost small in the distance. There overboard and bogging the deep fluffy mud here at low tide. The same deep fluffy mud that so testifies that Mud River is correctly named. Herb's big work skiff dried out and looking forlorn there resting on the mudflat not far from him. But what is Herb doing working his oysters when it will be a couple of months before he has sales for them? Then you see that he is bent over and with both hands pulling and tearing so he is knocking down and scattering the deadshell that always happen during late summer when oysters suffer a fifty percent mortality because of the continuous harsh heat and the continuous spawning that very often stresses them to death. So Herb is cleaning up his beds just as any responsible farmer would weed his fields. More free labor that hopefully will payoff later. But Herb does sell a damn fine bushel of oysters in the fall and the winter. But they are cluster oysters rather than single oysters. But Herb culls the clusters of all the deadshell until he has a much larger than your hand fan shaped cluster of two or three or four thick long oysters. And they are so salty with the good twice a day seawater flush that the beds get this close to Sapelo Inlet. And they are pearly and plump and healthful what with the still pristine water this far from the highlands and this close to the sea. Now Herb looks up and then straightens up at the low throbbing sound of a passing trawler in the distance that has disturbed this his summer evening working solitude. Now he recognizes Mustang and right away he recognizes you here waving big to him from her sterndeck. So with his two heavily gloved hands out stretched he waves back big also because yesterday you had told him about you all going to shrimp fish South Carolina.

CHAPTER SEVEN

The northern end of Sapelo Island and the southern end of St. Catherines Island seem much closer together and far more dangerous as you all go through the Inlet at low tide with Mustangs' long outriggers down and appearing to reach for the churning swirling water at the ends of these very old barrier islands. The sun gets larger now as it sets into the western horizon, so you turn on the light and right away the galley seems more cheerful. At the dock Johanna had passed across two foil covered trays of a half fried chicken each and corn seasoned with butter and string beans seasoned with bacon, and now you put these into the warmer and then pour iced tea into tall plastic glasses. Forrest is patiently keeping Mustang heading east for the long while that it will take to clear the far outstretching bars and shoals that go out from St. Catherine's ragged southern end for a long ways. And right away the heavy slow moving swells from the northeast begin to push against and then run under Mustangs' left side and so you all begin an exaggerated from one side to the other side roll and back. But finally now well clear of the far outstretching bars and shoals Forrest swings Mustang east of north, and right away the exaggerated rolling stops and an exaggerated up and up and over and over and down and down begins as the heavy slow moving swells run under and behind again and again.

Now you and Forrest are seated in the side by side high pedalested Captains' chairs that have such a commanding view way to the sides as well as across Mustangs' bow and out into the almost full dark now with Tybee light and then St. Helena Sound up there so far ahead. And in between a mouth full of chicken and a mouth full of corn, Forrest says, "Johanna said that Carol is living with you now." And in between a mouth full of string beans and a long pull of tea, you say, "yeah, when she isn't visiting her Dad in Brunswick." But Forrest only says, "huh," in reply. And once again you clearly feel the dislike that the people around here feel for her. And you assume that it is because her Dad and Brother were long known shrimp thieves. But as unfair as this broad blame is to Carol, you have never cared what these people feel about anything and you are not about to start now.

Then later, with the supper things cleaned and stowed away and the galley now dark and idle, with nothing but black night all around ahead outside and the green instrument lights all around here inside of the wheelhouse and with the National Weather Service continuous weather broadcast low in the background, Forrest says from his pedalested chair, "still going with us to Mexico?" And from your pedalested chair you say, "sure, if you all get the license." Then you add, "but remember that I don't speak Spanish, and that I sure as hell don't want to get boarded by bandidos." Because there isn't any need now in going into what all Herb had said. Because five thousand dollars a week is a whole lot of money. So there isn't any need in closing that door slam shut way too soon. Because there still is a chance, even though it is a slim chance, that they will somehow get the license. So you can say yes now, because you can always say no later.

You have been onboard fishing boats for so long now that you can get a good snooze anywhere and anytime and even a storm has to be a pretty terrible storm indeed for you not to be able to get a good snooze when a good snooze is called for and when a good snooze is much needed. So when your eyelids continue to flutter shut and when your eyes continue to roll back in your head and when your head continues to fall back suddenly and snap you awake once again, you just scrunch further down on your back in the Captains' chair and you better brace your feet forward against Mustangs' endless up and up and over and over and down and down the heavy slow moving swells and you drop your chin on your chest and you close your eyes restfully and you simply begin a good snooze. The automatic pilot is on and the continuous weather broadcast is low in the background and the green instrument lights are dim and pleasant here in this well after midnight now night with you all seven miles off shore and plenty wide east of Tybee light.

Then Forrest suddenly hollers, "there!!" But his voice is much too loud and far too shrill.

So you suddenly become fully awake now and you look and there slashing across Mustangs' bow from right to left and coming up fast from the deep trough of a swell as you all are going down the side of the same swell is the ghostly silver and black sailboat of Forrests' worst nightmare fears. Her sails are set and she is fully

69

rigged and she is crewless and she shimmers an evil light and she is terrifying. And just as suddenly she has slashed by left and is gone on by.

But then ahead, and just as suddenly, the heavy swell height is parted and there is only the enormous red bulbous cutwater bow of an even more enormous and towering high freighter that suddenly now absolutely fills all of Mustangs' windshield forward. And you hear yourself begin to holler, "Forrest!!" and in the corner of your eye you see him panic spinning the wheel hard right. But now there is only the drunken up and up feeling of Mustang rolling up and up. Then the drunken feeling of over and over. Then the drunken feeling of down and down. As she and you and you all are helplessly caught, catastrophically caught, in the freighters' truly enormous bow wake.

Then all and everything becomes absolute chaos. Because suddenly your world becomes an even more terrifying one of a terrible blow to the side of your head, and the brilliant shafts of light and the bursting showers of sparks that this brings. Then the plunged black underwater feeling of being hit and smashed from everywhere by sharp hard things. And the deafening underwater deep sounds of pings and whines and whooses and pops. And the utterly helpless underwater deep feeling of being caught ragman like in the powerful currents and throws of an endless gigantic whirlpool. Then huge streams of airless foamy bubbles quickly pass before you here in your now airless underwater deep terrifying world. Because there is no longer an up or a down or a sideways in any direction whatsoever, here suspended and flung and torn and tossed and lost and drowned for sure for sure for goddamn sure. Because now your lungs have long been screaming. But their scream is only one scream among a thousand screams.

That now become a pounding. But their pound is only one pound among a thousand pounds. Then the once every second and deafening Whoose! Whoose! Whoose! that now has overridden all of the other harsh sounds here in your deep underwater world eases its pound. And instantly you realize that the Whoose! Whoose! is not saying Whoose! Whoose! It is saying Son! Son! Then you see your Mom here deep underwater before you. And her deep underwater sweet face is horribly distorted in screaming Son! Son! Son!

And the breath that you take at long long last is loud and it is drenched and it is pitiful and it is desperate. But there is air among the seawater now. Actual air, real air, so very precious air. But now there is the coughing and the burning and the gagging and the spitting also. But more and more now there is the actual air, the real air, the so very precious air. So you grab onto the large bulky thing that is gently bumping your head and shoulders here seawater afloat now at long long last, here in this late dark night and under a billion overhead stars.

At first you are only aware of the close by splash and ripple and tickle of the seawater about your head and face. Then you become aware of the huge huge silence that is beyond and all around now. Then you feel a big northeast swell quietly raise you and raise you, then carry you and carry you, then quietly drop you and drop you, as it passes beneath and goes on by. And at the height of the raise you can see the nearby shattered and scattered parts of Mustang that are now collecting themselves into a debre trail. So you yell, "Forrest!" But the yell does not seem to travel very far out into the huge all around silence that is beyond.

Now you know that this large bulky thing that you have been clutching so frantically is one of the foam partition walls that separated the shrimp hold into bins. And by submerging one side and kicking your feet hard and reaching stretching far, you grab the other side. Now you are up onto the floating wall and out of the seawater. At the start of the next rise you get onto you knees, and at the top of the rise you cup your hands and yell, "Forrest!" But as the drop continues, there is still only silence here in the all around darkness. Then drifting whiffs of eiry before morning fog begin to quickly pass by. Then suddenly a dense fog bank moves in and is all around. But this dense fog is cold and wet so you begin to shiver. So you quickly take off your fishing boots and socks, and wring out the socks and put them back on. Then you take off your jeans and shorts, and wring them and put them back on. Then you do the same to your long sleeve flannel shirt and short sleeve cotton shirt. Then you dump the water from your fishing boots and put them back on. But you are still cold shivering wet. But cold and wet defines commercial fishermen as well as broke and haggard does. So nothing is new. And your clothes will dry eventually. And with the coming sunrise you will begin to warm. Then later in the morning you will become far too hot. So nothing is new still. Because from one extreme to the other extreme and feast or famine as well are mixed up in the definition of commercial fisherman also.

So you orient yourself here in the dense fog and darkness to the constant swells that are still running from the northeast to the southwest still heavy and slow and without end. So facing the swells, anywhere ahead and to the left is land. And anywhere behind and to the right is open ocean. But there is little comfort in this small knowledge. Because there is not one goddamn thing that you can do with this knowledge. Or about this your helplessly adrift predicament. Here foodless and waterless and toolless. As well as oarless and sailless and rudderless. But there really is some comfort in this vague knowledge of knowing in general where insignificant you is floating adrift here in this overwhelming in every direction seawater world. There really is. So you take this some comfort and you wisely use it to wrap yourself in to warm yourself with its hope as best as you can.

Now the fog bank passes as suddenly as it had arrived. Now there are the high and lonely billion stars again. Still there is only huge silence to your hoarse yells of, "Forrest!" Then the drifting eiry fog patches drift passed again. Then the billion stars shining high again. Then the deeper darkness that is always just before dawn. Then the quick lightening, lightening, lightening more that is the beginning of dawn itself. Now there is the glorious rim of the sweet, sweet sun that is splashes of reds and yellows and blues now. There is sweet light and sweet warmth and sweet hope that is rising fast, coming fast now. There, too, is Forrest! There! There to the southeast! There much farther seaward. He is seated in what looks like the big plastic sterndeck cooler. And he is bobbing and slowly revolving with it because it is much more effected by the variable and gusty northeast wind than down here so close to the sea surface you. And on one of his slow revolutions when you both are at the height of your separate swells rise he sees your frantic waving, and he waves back frantically also. Oh how wonderful. Oh how sweet. Because now you are not totally alone here on this overwhelming seawater world. Then for a long time you all wave at each other on each of his slow revolutions when your separate swells are at their height. Then suddenly as if by agreement you all stop waving. And now when the swells height and your revolutions meet, you all simply helplessly look at each other pitifully. Because the distance between you all continues to increase. Because gradually Forrest and the cooler have become smaller and smaller and smaller still. Until now, finally, you no longer can see them. And the sudden rush of terror and loneliness is staggering. So you wipe away the tears that have begun.

Now it is the middle of the morning. And the glare and the heat and the humidity are really fierce once again. Just as they were yesterday and the day before, and every day last week for weeks now of this typical Georgia summer. But you have been intensely following the black smoke trail of a ships' exhaust as it has slowly proceeded on its course just below the horizon there farther to the southeast. And as the suspense has increased, so has the beating of your heart. Then, Yes! Yes! Because when it gets to the direction where you last saw Forrest, the exhaust stops. The exhaust simply stops. And for long minutes now there is no exhaust. And for these long minutes you hold your breath as your heart continues to beat a mile a minute. Then suddenly there is the much blacker thicker exhaust of the ships' getting underway again. So you loudly whoop and holler and laugh because Forrest has been rescued.   Then you eagerly continue to follow the black smoke trail until it finally disappears just below the horizon there to the southeast. But now you begin to wonder about you. But what about me?   Well, what about you?   Seriously, what about me? Whatever happens, happens, is what about you. Whether soon rescued also, or a very slow dieing to death, or something dramatic in between, that's what about you. And there is not one goddam thing that you can do about it one way or the other. All you can do is to withdraw into the strong stamina reserve that a fisherman must have to simply hold on until whatever happens, and when.

Because if you are wrong about Forrests' rescue, it will not be until sometime tomorrow before David Sorenson begins to get concerned about you all not showing up at St. Helena Sound as planned. But first he will phone Johanna to see whether you all have called in a breakdown. Then he will phone all the docks and marinas in between. But even without a storm or a gale, anything can still happen to delay or to slow down a boat on a trip. And it usually does, and David knows that well. So David will continue to give you all the benefit of the doubt for awhile longer. So it will be much later still after that before he becomes finally concerned enough to go ahead and phone the Coast Guard. And only then will all of them begin to search these five hundred square miles of open ocean sameness here where you all could possibly be.

Now it is the middle of the afternoon and you have long been sitting cross-legged and patient here on the partition wall and waiting for whatever and when. Earlier you had taken off your flannel shirt and had hung it loose over your head and shoulders and arms like a small tent against the direct sun and its harsh glare off the all around water. But here under the shirt tent, the hot humidity is stifling. Outside there is the endless rise and the endless drop of the endless northeast swells. Outside there is the endless lap and tickle of the seawater wavelets against the partition wall. But here under the shirt tent with your head bowed against the stiffling humidity, there is also the throbbing constant pain of the raw gashed bump on your forehead above your left eye. And there are the hundred hurts from the hundred bruises and scrapes and cuts that are spread out evenly over the rest of your body until your entire body is one big hurt that hurts badly. And so you continue to wait patiently here for whatever and when.

But in your mind, you and your brother Tommy have the Mary Margaret anchored off Shell Castle, off Ocracoke. And it is a cool clear spring evening with a soft sea breeze blowing. And you all have caught plenty of shrimp in the deep hole that is inside the huge question mark shaped Royal Shoal. And now you and

Tommy are sitting leaned back on lawn chairs on the sterndeck with your feet casually up on the rail. Far beyond, the sun is slowly setting red redder reddest into gentle Pomplico Sound. And you all are drowsily happy and full after the thick ribeye steaks smothered in onions and mushrooms with fries oh so golden brown and crisp and well salted and the big salads globbed real good with creamy mayonaise. And after taking a long pull of cold beer, you hold the frosty bottle cold to your hot forehead. But from somewhere close by someone says, "hey, Cap. Hey, Cap, you all right?"

So you raise the shirt tent. And there dead in the water and calmly rocking here beside you on the partition wall is a snapper boat. And the three guys onboard are looking down at you in utter astonishment. So you say, "huh? What?"

CHAPTER EIGHT

"Herb. It's Ben." But the frantic activity in the background is loud as the Coast Guard people get geared up to do what they do so well. So you close your other ear with your finger so you can hear on the phone.

"What's wrong, Ben? Where are you?"

"Tybee Island Coast Guard Station. Look, Herb, we lost Mustang. A freighter coming into Savannah ran us over and never even knew it."

"Good God, no!"

"I think Forrest was picked up by another freighter, though, but I'm not sure. They're calling all the ships in the area now to see, and starting a search just in case."

"Good God, no, Ben! Are you hurt?"

"Pretty banged up and sore all over. They want me to go to the hospital at least overnight. But I want to get back to my place. Would you come get me?"

"Of course, Ben. I'll head out the door now, and be there as soon as possible. Should I call Johanna?"

"I just did. She's calling David Sorenson at St. Helena, and the guys around down there. Everyone will be out searching at first light tomorrow. But I think Forrest was picked up. Look, I hate to bother you with this. But I called Carol. But she still isn't at my place."

"Don't be silly, Ben.   I'm heading out the door now. Bye."

So with the frantic activity still loud in the background, you close your eyes and you try to collect yourself and to settle yourself for the next call.

As soon as the phone rings there, your Mom picks it up and says, "Son."

"Mom, I heard you."

"I know, Son. I told your Dad that you were all right."

So you say, "Mom." But then the tears begin to flood rush as the terror of the sinking becomes so very real once again.

"I know, Son. But you are safe now. You did not refuse the sea. And you are safe now. I told your Dad and Tommy to go ahead and go fishing this morning. That you were all right and that you would be picked up. They will be in in several hours, call back then. They will want to talk to you."

So you say that you will and that Herb, the oysterman friend of yours from Southport, is coming to get you and take you to your place. And that you will call home then. Then you say that you think Forrest was picked up.

But your Mom is only silent. Finally she says, "he was, Son, but his people won't hear from him for a long while."

So Herb continues to listen as he has you all out of Savannahs' traffic and now up onto Interstate 95 and heading south. So you get another beer from the cooler and then you continue your rambling talk. "That silver and black sailboat is real,

Herb. I saw it. I did. It saved our lives, Herb. It did. The freighter would have run over us and we would be drowned. But somehow the sailboat woke Forrest in time for him to swerve in time. The radar was on. But we dozed and didn't give a thought to crossing the shipping lanes. I mean Savannah is a busy port. But not that busy. I mean what are the odds of a collision? I guess we assumed that they would look out for us. But maybe they were also dozing. I mean that is a huge area of open ocean. I mean what are the odds, Herb? But Forrests' ghost sailboat is real, Herb. It sure as hell is. I saw it. I did. It sliced across right before Mustangs' bow. All sleek and clean and crewless. She is fully rigged and sailing herself, Herb. I saw her. I did. No wonder Forrest is terrified of her. Nothing has ever terrified me, Herb, nothing, ever. But she terrified me, Herb. How can she be out there sailing herself, Herb, appearing and disappearing so suddenly, so mysteriously? She sliced by, then there wasn't anything ahead but the huge red bulbous cutwater of the freighter pushing a huge roll of bow wake. Forrest swerved Mustang into that huge roll. But then terror became horror just that quickly, Herb. Because right away we knew that Mustang was lost. I've never lost a boat, Herb. I've never been onboard a lost boat. We lost Mustang, Herb. We did. We truly did. Beautiful, beautiful, hard working Mustang. Forrest swerved, she rolled, then she just came apart, Herb. Like a stick boat, Herb. Her big heavy rib timbers became just sticks, Herb." But now you begin to have the jerks and the starts and the shivers and the panics of actually being underwater once again and once again surrounded by the churning wreckage and the pain and the terror and the horror. So Herb looks from the road to you with sudden concern. So you try to shake away these too real again feelings and images. But they are too real, again. So you say, "I've never before known terror and horror well, Herb. But I do not want to know terror and horror well, Herb." Then, finally, and in a small voice, you say, "we lost Mustang, Herb. We lost poor lost Mustang, Herb. We truly did."

But there is not anything that Herb can say. So Herb does not say anything. So for this time you all are just one more vehicle among the very many fast traveling vehicles that are southbound in the night on Interstate 95.

Then you all come down the off ramp, then turn east onto the narrow state road. And now you all are back among the pine trees and the marshes and the live oaks and the hanging moss and the shacks and the rural poverty of McIntosh County of commercial fishing and pulpwood logging that breeds its own special kind of vicious redneck. So you tell Herb about your Moms' face yelling, "Son! Son!" and how that saved you when you were certainly lost. And about your phone call to her. And about her saying, yes, that Forrest was picked up. But that his people would not hear from him in a long while. And after moments of again looking at you with sudden concern, Herb says, "Ben, you might should keep that part to yourself."

Then in the night in your sleep you wake yourself with your low moans of, oh, oh, oh, from the pain of all the cuts and the bruises and the scrapes. So you gently change positions. But there is not any position that is without pain. So you simply accept the hurting all over and you relax yourself to it, and then your low moans of oh, oh, oh, become a soothing comfort.

Then in the night in your sleep Carols' warm lips are cool on your feverish face. And her soft hair falls about your face with the scent of her. And her tender words and her cool hands and her warm kisses and her wet tears become a soothing comfort also. "Are you hurt badly, baby? How badly are you hurt, baby? My brave brave hurt baby, my so brave hurt baby. I'm here now, baby. Now. Now, I'm here now sweet baby. Now, now, sleep, sleep now sweet brave baby, I'm here now. Oh, my so hurt, Ben, my so hurt, Ben."

But in the early morning in the steamed bathroom mirror as you carefully shave around the hurts, Carols' face is an angry reflection over your shoulder and her words are angry as well. "Ben, you cannot go, I will not allow you to go. You are hunt too badly, and you should stay in bed or at least rest on the couch. Ben, you cannot help in the search, and you can only hurt yourself more. I will not allow you to go."

So you say, "Carol, this does not have anything to do with you. I have never before lost a boat. And I have never before lost a Captain. Then in a second I lost both boat and Captain. So I must be a part of the search. I must. If I am not much help in the search, at least I am a part of the search. I must be a part of the search, Carol."

So when you step onboard Princess at the dock at the grey beginning of dawn, Red and then Johnny come and shake your hand. Then Mike and his following behind bulldog buddy Petey come, and Mike shakes your hand. Then Johanna steps on board Princess, and right away she comes and gives you a big long hug. But by the time Red has Princess passing through Sapelo Inlet, you are already in a bunk. And with the engine noise hiding your low moans of oh, oh, oh, you pass into sleep.

Then in the afternoon, you are sitting at the table in the galley and you are eating the tomato soup and the grilled cheeze sandwich that Johanna fixed for you. And once again Johanna asks you to tell her about last seeing Forrest. So once again you tell her how he was kneeling in the large deck cooler, and how you all frantically waved to each other across the increasing distance, whenever your separate swell heights met and whenever the cooler revolutions had him facing you. Then how you all finally stopped waving, and how you all then just helplessly looked at each other, whenever the swell heights and the revolutions met. Then once again you tell her how the freighter exhaust smoke on the horizon trailed behind until it got to where Forrest would have drifted, and how it then stopped and began to drift up. And then how after many minutes, the exhaust smoke suddenly became darker blacker thicker and then how it began to drift behind again now that the freighter was underway again. And all of this time Johanna is standing with her back against the counter and she is intently watching you and she is carefully listening to your every word. She has her arms crossed on her chest with the fingers of one hand covering her mouth, and her eyes are wide and they are wet and tears go quickly down her cheeks. But you do not tell Johanna what your Mom said.

Then in the morning of the next day, David Sorensen radios Red to say that one of his guys from Edisto Island has picked up the piece of the cooler wall that you had floated on. Then in the afternoon the Coast Guard radios that one of their aircraft has spotted the large deck cooler that Forrest had kneeled in, and that a vessel is on its way to pick it up. But that Forrest is not in or anywhere around the cooler. Then late in the afternoon the Coast Guard radios again that they have completed contacting all the ships along the southeast coast, but that none of the ships report picking up Forrest. And after a long stunned silence in Princesses' wheelhouse with you and Johanna and Johnny and Mike standing around, Red angrily radios back that that is impossible that you had seen a ship stop on the horizon where Forrest would have been. Then the Coast Guardsman replies that he is well aware of your report, and that in addition to the surface search, they have proceeded with the investigation that Forrest has been rescued. But that no ship reports picking him up. So Red fires back to stop and search all the ships. But after a pause the Coast Guardsman patiently replies that they are not authorized to arbitrarily stop and search international shipping. And that would be physically impossible even if they were, because by now the southeast coast ships are intermingling with the northeast coast ships to the north and with the Caribbean and the Gulf of Mexico ships to the south. And that there is no way of telling which are which or which were which. So Red holds the radios' microphone away from his mouth with his finger off the key, and he looks around the wheelhouse at you all for a suggestion. Finally, you shrug resigned and say to just ask them to check once again and make certain that they contact all the ships that could have been anywhere near here. And after Red does that, the Guardsman replies that they are in the process of doing that now and will let him know the results. But you all already know the results of that. And once again a stunned silence becomes thick here in the wheelhouse. And once again Johanna's fingers go up and cover her mouth and her eyes become wide and wet, and now tears begin going down her cheeks. So you and Mike and Johnny and Red find somewhere else to look so none of you can see that your eyes are wet also. Because now Forrest is truly lost at sea. He truly is, for sure, for sure.

At noon of the next day the Guardsman radios Red that they will call off their air and surface search at sundown. But right away David Sorensen radios that he and the Edisto Island guys will continue the search for another day if Red wants. And Red replies, yeah, thanks guys. And one boat at the time, the McIntosh County guys radio that they will continue searching also. And again Red says thanks guys into the radio microphone. Then the long silence becomes as unendurable as the search has become unendurable.

And the slow single file line of McIntosh boats that finally comes back through Sapelo Inlet says it all without saying anything.

Because yet another commercial fisherman has become lost at sea. As so very many commercial fishermen have become lost at sea over the years. And as soon as you drive in the yard and get out of the truck, Carol is out of the house running and in your arms crying.

CHAPTER NINE

Then the next morning you go to the bank and you get a five hundred dollar signature loan. Because the lights and the water and the phone are about to be turned off. Because the rent is more than a month behind. Because you said no that you would handle it on the phone to your Dad the other night when he asked if you wanted him to send you some money. Because other than Carol helping out some on food, the bills are your responsibility.

Then you go to the Doctor and you tell him that it hurts when you breathe. And after he examines you he says well no damn wonder my friend what with you walking around with three cracked ribs and some fine cracks they are too. And when he tightly wraps your chest the hurts when you breathe eases considerably as long as you do not breathe too deeply. Then he puts several clamps in the swollen raw gash over your eye and as he is dressing it he says you will have some fine scar there my friend for a conversation starter because you did not get it attended to sooner. Then he says and on top of everything else you have some fine concussion there my friend and my advice, which you won't take anyway, is that you stay in bed for a few days. But the good news is that all of your other bangs and bongs and so forth are coming along nicely though. So you go home and you lie on the couch and for the rest of the day you thoroughly enjoy how much Carol thoroughly enjoys waiting on you so.

But early the next morning you are down at the dock helping Johanna get the boats iced and fueled and on their way shrimping finally after the long search. But their pulling away from the dock now is a hard reminder that you do not have a boat. And a fisherman without a boat is about as useless as a one legged man at an ass kicking contest. So you stand on the dock and you wave them goodbye with a bitter smile on your face anyway. Then you grit your teeth and you purse your lips and you simply deal with this knowing that now and for however long you do not have a boat.

So you busy yourself by assembling a hundred or more wood slat and wire seafood boxes for when the boats come in to unload. For when their fish and shrimp catches are packed out in ice in these seafood boxes and then trucked locally and medium distance and long distance to seafood wholesalers and to seafood distributors everywhere. Then you sweep out the packing house and then hose it down as well as all of its conveyors and equipment and machinery. Then you clean up and straighten up around the office. Then you pick up the trash along the dock and out into the parking area. Then you and Johanna sit facing each other from separate desks and have a late lunch in the office. But the silence that is between you all and through out the office and out into the deserted packing house and all along the deserted dock is unendurable it truly is for sure.

Because owning several boats and the packing house and the dock aside, she and Forrest had begun to be squeezed financially by the long summer lack of shrimp around here along with everyone else you included, or else Forrest never would have decided to go to South Carolina in search of shrimp what with his great fear of the ghost sailboat that you did not believe in that now you certainly do believe in. So now Johanna must deal with the huge not knowing that surrounds Forrests' being lost at sea. Which is not like he is dead and there is his body and once it is buried there is closure. Rather he is lost and at sea and there is no way of knowing whether he will ever be found. And she must deal with the practical responsibilities of keeping this their family business operating today and tomorrow and all of the days until Forrest is either found eventually or is never found ever. So Johanna simply cannot keep you on the payroll even at minimum wage for very long. Because while the cleaning up and the straightening up that you have done and will do is necessary, it is not needed daily or even weekly usually. And besides, you did not come all the way down here just to be the clean-up man at a seafood packing house. So when you lost Mustang, you lost your commercial fishermans' job. So now you are six hundred miles from home with very little money left from the signature loan and without a job and what the hell are you going to do now Ben? In spite of the fact that the other night on the phone your Dad said Ben come on home, Son, you know that Tommy and I need you on the Mary Margaret or the Betty Fagan and it is foolish for us to hire strikers here for them when you are down there striking, and your Mom is missing you especially bad especially now that you have been ship wrecked and hurt and damn near drowned.   But you said Dad I came down here to see if I could make it on my own and if I leave and come home this soon I will never know whether I could have made it on my own and I want to see whether I can make it on my own.

But now you do not have a boat. So now you do not have a job.   And the other boats that you would work on, that are Captained by serious honest Captains, all have strikers that are capable enough and competent enough to handle their sterndecks single handed. Even though the first day of the search Red right away offered to have you double with Johnny on Princess and Johnny right away agreed. But you knew that Johnny could handle it without your halving his pay. Sure he would not mind it for a few days, a week, because good fishermen help each other that way when they can. But after a week of half pay Johnny would begin to mind it, and you would begin to mind it too if you were in his position. So what the hell are you going to do now Ben?

Then in the evening at the end of the week you and Carol are sitting down to supper but there is a knock on the door and when you go to the door you see that it is Mike. So you say hey Mike surprised that he has come to your home to see you when he has never done that before. And he says look, Ben, can we talk? And you say sure Mike come on in, Carol and I have just started supper come on in and eat with us. But he says no I'm sorry I disturbed your supper, Ben, I'll come back later. But you say don't worry about it, Mike, there's plenty. We packed out today and I brought home a bucket full of fresh mullet. It's nothing fancy, only fried mullet and grits and slaw. But there's plenty of it and Carols' a fine cook, and you're more than welcome, so come on in. So Mike says well I'm sick of my cooking that's for sure, and it sure sounds good if you all don't mind. So you say of course not come on in. Then you see Petey standing in the back of Mikes' truck with his front paws up on the side of the truck and carefully watching his best buddy Mike and what he is doing and where he is going and who he is talking with. So you say hey Petey how you doing and right away he recognizes your voice as friend so he gets a grin on his droopy sad happy bulldog face and his tail stump begins to wag furiously. And Mike says stay there Petey sternly and then comes in.

Then while Mike is sitting at the table and Carol is getting him a plate and knife and fork and a glass of tea, they speak casually to each other as people do who have grown up around each other. But you think you notice a moment of hesitancy in Mike in being in such close surroundings with Carol. But this hesitancy last only for a moment, so you wonder about it but you do not dwell on it. Then you all quickly become very busy at working on the fried mullet and grits and slaw and for this while the only talk is please pass the mullet or have some more slaw or need more tea.

Then later you all are sitting back in your chairs and wiping your hands and your mouths with napkins. So Mike leans forward in his chair and says, look Ben, why I came by, Don Arbo down at Golden Isle Seafood on St. Simons Island called to see if I would Captain a boat that he is bringing up from their dock down at St.

Augustine to shrimp off here this fall. The crew that has been working her doesn't want to leave their homes and families for that long so Don needs a crew here. I was a striker on one of Dons' boats that shrimped the Gulf last year so Don knows me. I told Don about the mess with Slicer and the Sea Warrior and he said yeah that he heard about it but he isn't concerned about it and he still wants me to Captain this boat. Ben, you know that a lot of the guys around here still hold that sinking against me, and that I've been having a hard time getting on another boat around here. And I know that you have been standing up for me whenever anyone has said anything bad about me, and I really appreciate that, Ben, I really do, and I stopped by to see if you would strike for me on this boat. Then Mike holds up his hand and says wait before you say no, let me finish, I know that you have more Captain experience than me and that you are better qualified to Captain this boat than me, but Don knows me and he doesn't know you even though he has heard of you. Then Mike holds up his hand again and says wait Ben, let me finish, its the usual deal, expenses off the top, then his share is fifty percent and we share fifty percent. Wait, officially I'll be Captain and you'll be striker, but between us we'll take turns and work the boat like equal partners fifty fifty. Then red faced Mike sits back in the chair and is breathing hard from saying so much so quickly.

So you laugh loud and you smile big and you say what I've been trying to say Mike is hell yes, anything to get back on a boat. I need a boat like a dead man needs a coffin. Carol and I have been fussing with each other all week because I've been so hard to live with because I've been so worried about getting on another boat. Just before you came we were talking about my having to go back home if I didn't get on another boat soon, and was Carol coming with me or not. Then you say, Mikes' a godsend, isn't he Carol, and you reach and put your hand over her hand on the table. And she says, yes you are Mike, thank you, and she is smiling big at Mike. But now Mike is embarrassed and so his face gets red for that reason. So you say your split is damn generous Mike but you know I'll take less just to get back on a boat. But Mike says, no, equal partners like I said, Ben, but let's really bust ass working this boat and go where we have to go and do what we have to do to keep her loaded with shrimp all of this fall because I've enjoyed as much poverty as I can stand and I really mean that. And smiling grimly as you remember all the long summer months of a handful of shrimp a handful of shrimp that was then followed by the loss of Mustang and Forrest that meant the loss of your job, you look Mike in the eyes and you say you have yourself a deal Mike you sure as hell do.

Then Mike says, oh, the best part or the worst part, however you want to look at it, the name of the boat is the Silly Sally. Then he laughs. Then you and Carol laugh and say together, Silly Sally, really? And he nods big and says yeah, laughing. Then Mike says and the boat I worked on for Don last year in the Gulf is named the Bossy Bonnie, and another of his boats is named the No Brain Lorraine. Well, now all three of you are guffawing so hard that tears have come to your eyes. Then in between guffaws and wiping away tears Carol says lordy lordy Don or whoever names his boats hasn't been having any kind of good luck with women. So the good mood and the laughter and the tears continue and they are a godsend too. Because all of a sudden things are not so desperate and things are not so sad and things are not so unendurable.

So several days later Carol drives you and Mike down to the Golden Isle Seafood dock on St. Simons Island so you all can bring Silly Sally up here to Johannas' dock. But on the trip up the inland waterway you all soon see that she has not been properly maintained and that some of her equipment is pretty run down and that some of her gear is so frayed that it is dangerous. So when you all get tied to Johannas' dock Mike goes into the office and calls Don and says look Don and the rest of it, to which Don answers okay you're right I see and so forth, until finally he says you all do what you have to Mike to get her right and send me the bill but get to shrimping as soon as you all can hear? So now you and Mike spend the next days in hard work free labor and by the end of the third day you all have Silly Sally cleaned and maintained and refitted and ship shape properly. Until she is really proud of herself and she looks it. Until you all are really proud of her and you show it. Until the endless wise cracks about her name by the wise guys all along the dock and out into the parking lot become a source of pride as well.

Then the next day you and Mike go to Foodland to get the

food and drinks and supplies for a four day trip shrimp fishing. And while Mike is signing the on account of we're broke tab at the checkout counter that says in effect we will absolutely positively pay you in full when we get back in and have the shrimp that we surely hopefully surely catch packed out and paid for, you glance at the shuffling impatiently line that has formed while you all got the two chocked slam full shopping carts of stuff checked out. And there at the end of the line as calm and unconcerned as ever is Georgia McIntosh! So right away you hear yourself gasp and you feel your head become light and you feel something in your chest go thump bump. Because once again she is so blonde beautiful and so clothes sophisticated. So you feel your legs start to give way also. But she does not look at you. But right away you know that she had been looking at you intently. But she knows that you are looking at her. So now she will not look at you.

CHAPTER TEN

So you all bring Silly Sally out of Doboy Inlet and stay wide of the long shoal behind which Sea Warrior came aground and broke apart and head southeast and gradually more south. And just like the scene of any big accident it is impossible not to look and so you all do look and sure enough there are portions of the hull and portions of the outriggers sticking up out of the sand and the surf and the spray. So you look at Mike and Mike looks at you. Then he purses his mouth grimly and he shakes his head sadly but he does not speak. So you all look across Silly Sallys' bow. And you all hope that down there to the south things will be better.

Because to a commercial fisherman there is no glory in the loss of his boat whatever the reason whatever the cause. And whether right or wrong or fair or not there is a shame that is attached to the loss of his boat that is greater than any other shame and more longer lasting than any other shame. And whether this is right or wrong or fair or not, this is so.

But during the night a large cold front quickly pushed its artic express way from the midwest into the southeast. And with the arrival of this cold front the temperature suddenly thudded to the lower forties. So fall gave her wake up call her tap on the shoulder her oh youhoo call this morning saying that she is near nearer that she is fast coming that she is soon arriving. As she says hey remember me? Saying you thought I had forgotten about you but I hadn't forgotten about you sweet cheeks. Saying remember how numbing chilling shivering I can be? Saying you all have been cursing the heat for all of these long summer months so how does the shock of these late September lower forties grab you? Numbing aren't they? Chilling aren't they? Shivering aren't they? Especially this so suddenly after the endless hot hot hot that you all thought would never end that you all thought would go on forever. Saying and you all have forgotten about my fall northeasters as well, haven't you? Sure you have. How once I get my winds into the northeast I blow them strong stronger and cold colder from there for three days or for six days or for nine days always in threes you see as all fishermen know. Because northeast is my particular favorite direction because it is your least favorite direction. Saying but not yet for a northeaster, soon yes, but not yet for a northeaster. Because in a day or two I will move this cold front much farther southeast and far off shore so more hot can move in behind it from the southwest. Saying I just wanted to take this opportunity to remind you that I will be very much a part of what is in store for you for the months to come. Aren't you glad? Aren't you just jumping up and down with joy? Of course you are. I knew you would be. But the good news is that with my arrival the water temperature will begin to drop and that will stir the main schools of shrimp out of the creeks and into the rivers. Then as the water temperature continues to drop these schools will stir from the rivers and into the sounds. Until finally they begin to stir out of the sounds

97

and through the inlets and into the ocean where you all will be hoping upon hope for a good fall shrimp run and therefore a profitable season. And I wish you good luck with these hopes of yours. But do not forget to bring the perseverance and the stamina that is as necessary and as equally important as good luck if not more so. Because you will surely need them. Or have you forgotten that also?

So for the next several days you and Mike and Petey too of course gradually work your way south in search of the stray pockets the shifting drifts of shrimp wherever they might be and sometimes are. In the troughs in the holes along the beaches along the sandbars in the deeps in the shallows. Looking and trying here looking and trying there, with a coastal chart spread out on the galley table with you and Mike standing and pondering over it pointing discussing deciding the next hole to try the next beach or trough or bar or deep or shallow to try. Turning for another pass through when there is a decent amount of shrimp in a trawl. Moving more south still when there is not. St. Simons Island and Jekyll Island and Cumberland Island and Fernandina and Little Talbot and then the long stretch of beach from Jacksonville to St. Augustine. And it is great fun and pure joy and it is hard work and long hours as you and Mike take turns at Captaining the wheel and take turns at culling the sterndeck. Because you are back on a workboat again finally. Because you are back at the job that you know the best and love the most.

But you continue to have the sudden moments of sheer

terror as you once again see the vivid flashes of the slicing by from right to left silver and black sailboat then the huge red bulbous freighters' cutwater that fills Mustangs' windshield forward then the slams and the pounds and the furies of being in the water and under the water in swirls and tows of pings and pops and bams and whams during the wrecking the breaking up the shattering. And for these solitary private moments you jerk and fit and sweat and goosebump with the same terror returned. Because to be a commercial fisherman over time in the most dangerous profession of all professions by far is to collect your own personal collection of close calls and worst nightmares and oh shits. But you handle these terror moments and you deal with these terror moments, and thereby you learn to live with these terror moments. But you do not refuse the sea, ever.

So Mike gets on the radio to Don Arbo up at Golden Isles Seafood and says Don we're just north of St. Augustine and the good news is that we have a thousand maybe twelve hundred pounds of mostly thirties count and the rest forties count and we haven't spared the ice so they are in damn good shape even after four days. And right away Don answers great Mike great, you and Ben have done great, I knew you all would. Thirties are bringing well over four dollars a pound and forties down close to three dollars so all of us will have a good payday, great news Mike so what's the bad news? And Mike answers well the end of the portside outrigger bent on the last trawl just now not bad but bad enough. And Don answers no problem Mike you all just go on to my dock down there. I'll phone so they'll know you all are coming and to get a welder to come over and straighten the outrigger until we can replace that section. And Mike go ahead and pack out there and reice and refuel and then what Mike? And Mike says well we'll work our way back up just like we did coming down it worked once maybe it'll work again. And Don says, great, ten to twelve boxes in late September is damn good news Mike, you fellas have done damn good Mike! So Mike says thanks Don, me and Ben are feeling pretty damn proud of ourselves too.

Now it is well into the afternoon and the slanting sun what with the shorter days now is warm and furry and satisfying with you and Mike sitting relaxed in lawn chairs on Dons' long dock where it tees with Silly Sally tied up beside you all all cocked over like a wounded wing duck with her port side outrigger laying along the tee part that goes to the packing house with the welder out at the bent end framing and banging and cussing and sweating and otherwise doing whatever it is that welders do to straighten bent outrigger ends. And after you all had packed out and iced and fueled and the trip expense tally tallied, you and Mike had shared out just over nine hundred dollars each for the catch after expenses, so talk about big shit eating grins there were two prime examples of big shit eating grins on your faces for sure. So you all got one of the guys who works at the dock to take you all in his truck to the grocery so you all could restock there for the return trip and especially beer because beer is so much cheaper down here and of course two whopping ribeye steaks for a celebration tonight that you all well earned well deserved and you all know it. But when you phoned Carol with the good news great news the phone just went on ringing and ringing and ringing up there in your empty house in McIntosh County.

Then across cocked over wounded wing duck Silly Sally you all see a trawler coming up the wide creek and beginning its turn to the dock. And in the turn the striker is at the sterndeck rail waving and the Captain is leaning out of the wheelhouse door waving and they are both hollering Silly Sally is back Silly Sally is back our sister ship is back! And after the slow turn and the hard reversing in and the soft bump against the dock you and Mike see that she is the No Brain Lorraine. So you all go help get her tied up and settled in. And by now the welder comes up wiping the grease and grime from his hands with a dirty rag and says okay fellas its as straightened as I can get it straightened and it should be straight enough until you can replace that section whenever. So all of you get the port side outrigger raised and locked and then retie Silly Sally so she doesn't look wounded wing duck looking any longer. Now you and Mike with Petey lying beside him and Alan and Buzzy from the No Brain Lorraine are sitting happy in lawn chairs on Silly Sallys' righted sterndeck and you all are well into some serious beer drinking and I mean some serious beer drinking indeed.

And since Buzzy takes his beer drinking even more seriously than the rest of you, it isn't long before all he can say is to murmur to himself and to anyone who cares to listen a repetition of fuzzy wassy was a bear fuzzy wassy had no hair fuzzy wassy wasn't fuzzy was he buzzy fuzzy wassy was a bear fuzzy wassy had no hair fuzzy wassy wasn't fuzzy was he buzzy fuzzy again and again. Then while Alan is telling you and Mike how the butterfly nets that they shrimp with in Louisiana are rigged and how they are used and how you just move ahead gradually against an outgoing or incoming tide with the butterfly nets down in the water on either side of the boat rather than trawled from the stern, Buzzy slowly slips from his lawn chair and gently slides full length to the deck. And in what is left of the warm furry satisfying setting of the sun, Buzzy hugs himself into a sleepy baby curl there on the sterndeck with his face resting on the palm of one hand and his juicy mouth burbling fuzzy then later wassy then later was and so on. So Petey raises his droopy jowl bulldog face and looks long at this pitiful specimen lying so close to him and burbling. Then with great indignation Petey gets up and goes and lies down on the other side of Mikes' chair and rests his droopy jowl face on his outstretched front paws and sighs deeply and then returns to his so sweet dreams of dancing bulldog bitches and other funs and frolics. Meanwhile you have been telling Mike and Alan the how tos and the why fors of channel netting shrimp at night in the main feeder creeks on a falling tide in Bogue Sound near Swansboro up in North Carolina. Because it has been a good day. Because it has been a great day. Because commercial fishing is all that you have ever done. Because commercial fishing is all that you ever want to do.

Now later Buzzy is still burbling away haltingly wetly but now in his bunk on the No Brain Lorraine and Alan is in his bunk and yelling across Jesus Christ Buzzy will you give it a goddamn rest so we can get some sleep because five o'clock is going to come mighty early! While Mike gives Petey the remnants of the two whopping ribeyes while you finish cleaning the supper things in Silly Sallys' galley.

Now you and Mike are settled again in the lawn chairs on Silly Sallys' sterndeck for one last beer here under billions of near far startling stars and a not long ago risen huge gorgeous moon. But the appreciation of the above panorama silence between you all goes on far too long until it becomes awkward and towards uncomfortable. Because in the corner of your eye you see Mike start to say something several times but each time noticeably stop himself. So you just wait for him to say whatever it is that he wants to say that he doesn't want to say. And now Mike suddenly braces himself and says in a rush look Ben this isn't any of my business and I try to mind my own business and I don't know if you know and it's only a rumor anyway and I've been telling myself to just stay out of it but we've become real good friends in the past week and if you don't know you should know that everyone in McIntosh County thinks that Carol is dealing cocaine in a big way and has been for some time.

CHAPTER ELEVEN

So when you push open the door a rush of November evening cold wind fills the almost empty Laughing Gull. So Herb turns on his stool from talking across to the bartender and says, "hey Ben, long time no see, but hurry and close that damn pneumonia hole, I've already enjoyed as much cold as I can stand for one day."

So you and Herb shake hands warmly and you say, "damn Herb, your hand is like ice." And Herb looks down at his red and white splotched and still puckered hands and says, "still numb, just got in from picking oysters, goes with the territory as you know." So you nod that you well know as you sit on the next stool and ask, "so were your Thanksgiving sales good?" And right away Herbs' warm smile vanishes as he shakes his head bad and grimaces his face disaster and says, "bad Ben, a real disaster. Thanksgiving week is always good, real good, as is Christmas week and New Years week. I mean you can always count on emptying a stuffed full to the ceiling cooler and stand there wishing you had another stuffed full to the ceiling cooler. Always. But the week before Thanksgiving thirty people got sick from bad oysters in Pensacola. Then several days later another twenty people got sick from bad oysters in Fort Lauderdale. And right away the press and television jumped on the bad news big time and rode it hard." And you nod that you had heard about it on the news as Herb continues, "and right away my phone stops ringing, Ben, I mean my sales just quit wham. Absolutely none after they started the 'eat oysters and die' shit." Now Herb gets a plea for understanding tone in his voice as he continues, "Ben you know that my leases are approved, that my harvesting is monitored, that my water quality is pristine, that my handling and cooler is checked. Ben, you know that there isn't a damn thing wrong with my oysters. But my oysters got painted with the same bad press brush as the bootlegged Florida oysters." And Herbs' so painful expression hurts you also. Now Herb shrugs in resignation and says, "I finally dumped the last fifty bushels off on a seafood wholesaler who was heading north and away from the bad press at below cost just to keep from getting stuck with them."

And again Herb shakes his head bad and grimaces his face disaster. So you say, "I'm sorry as hell, Herb, I know how much you needed a good sales week." So Herb looks at you with near tears in his eyes and says, "Ben you know there's not a damn thing wrong with my oysters." So you nod that you know. Just as you both know that this is just another reminder of the anquish of the desparate struggles under impossible obstacles that all good fisherman everywhere share.

But in the bar mirror you see that the rednecks have begun to shuffle in, in ones and twos for their usual night of drinking and shooting pool and shoving and bragging. And Herb continues in his depression, "well, it's over and done with now, and nothing can change it. It's three weeks until Christmas week and hopefully the

Florida bootleggers will stop picking in polluted waters. But probably not." Which leads to another bad head shake and disaster grimance. So to try to get Herb off this depressing conversation, you ask him whether his wife came down from Southport for Thanksgiving. But he sighs resigned and says, "yeah, but that became a disaster like everything else that week. All we did was argue, then she left several days early." And again Herb looks at you pleadingly. "Ben, the leases are in my name and the business is in my name, and I've invested too much time and money in them to just throw up my hands and walk away like she wants me to do. I can't admit failure no matter how bad things are."

And as bad as you feel about Herbs' bad sales week and his bad marriage and his bad other things, this conversation has become just too depressing, and a continuation of the reminder that to accept commercial fishing today is to accept desperate struggles under impossible obstacles as natural. So you abruptly say, "well, my trip home went great. Nothing cures homesickness like going home. And I actually didn't mind leaving to come back here. But Dad said that they will have the dock and packing house down at Sealevel finished by spring, and that I will, and he stressed 'will,' be back up working with them by then."

So right away Herb gets into this different conversation by saying, "you didn't mind coming back because you and Mike have been catching the hell out of shrimp lately."

And you quickly answer without apologizing, "yes we have, Herb, and making money changes everything. But Mike and I have put in long and I mean long hours shrimping, and we haven't stayed tied to the dock drinking beer and complaining about no shrimp out there."

And Herb looks up in the bar mirror at the rednecks bragging and shoving each other at the pool tables and says, "yeah, you all have definitely become the talk around here. That's for sure. But not good talk, Ben. You know how these people are. They don't like to see anyone doing better than they are. Especially when its deserved."

So again you quickly answer, "well screw these people, they don't pay my bills. Herb, there have been plenty of times when Mike and I worked most of the night at the dock to get Silly Sally patched up enough to be out shrimping in the morning. So screw these people. They can go to hell." And now there is cold anger in your voice.

So Herb holds up his hands in whoa don't get mad at me I'm just the messenger, and says, "I know, I know, I'm on your side, Ben, but there's more to it than you all catching more shrimp. A lot more. Ben, everyone is saying that you're the reason Mustang got sunk and Forrest got lost." So now you really flash mad. "What?! Me?!"

But Herb holds up his hands again in whoa. "Ben, they're saying that you knew that Forrest was terrified of the ghost sailboat and didn't want to go to South Carolina, but you kept hounding him until he went anyway." So you break in and say, "Herb, we were starving to death staying around here for a handful of shrimp a handful of shrimp, we had to go looking." So Herb breaks in, hands whoa, "I know, Ben, I know. But nothing has been heard from Forrest and it has been two months. And now they're saying that it is your fault."

"Herb, that's the silliest damn thing I've ever heard. Boats get sunk, men get lost, that just goes with the job. But the ghost sailboat is real, I know, I've seen it. And I still wake up in a cold sweat reliving the sinking. But I'm a shrimper, so I go shrimping, terrified or not. And there have been times when Mike and I have been trawling when I knew, I knew Herb, that the sailboat was out there somewhere close and closing fast, and it was all I could do to keep from jumping overboard and swimming to the beach. Herb, Forrest went to South Carolina because if he didn't go the Bank was going to take Mustang, not because I hounded him. Forrest was a shrimper, he had to go shrimping, that's all there was to it." But in the mirror you see Jerry Harrelson come in with one of his buddies, and right away you know that they are already drunk. So the back of your mind says, uh oh, trouble coming. And when Jerry sees you he elbows his buddy, and now they are both looking at you and grinning.

And even though Herb is also looking in the mirror, he goes on and says, "I know, Ben, you're right about Forrest. But there's still more. Mike was on Sea Warrior when she sank. You were on Mustang when she sank. Now you and Mike are together on Silly Sally. So everyone is taking bets on when you all will sink her. They are saying that you and Mike are boat sinkers, Ben."

So your jaw drops dumbfounded and you say, "oh Jesus, Herb, that's the silliest goddamn thing I've ever heard." But down the bar you hear the bartender tell Jerry and his buddy that he won't serve them, that they have had enough, that they can stay and shoot pool if they want, but only if they don't start trouble. And the back of your mind says that the trouble starting won't be long in coming now. But you go ahead anyway and say, "no one can seriously believe that Mike and I are boat sinkers, Herb."

But Herb shrugs and says, "but that's exactly what they believe, Ben. You know that these people have to have someone else to hate so they don't have to blame their failures on themselves. I'm only a bay fisherman to them, and therefore not a real commercial fisherman, so they talk openly around me as though I don't exist. So, Ben, you can believe me when I say that the talk is bad, real bad, and it gets worse everytime you and Mike dock with so much more shrimp than any other boat."

So your anger returns as you say, "well Mike and I aren't going to start dumping shrimp overboard just because we are making every one else look bad."

But Herb again holds up his hands in whoa I'm just the messenger and says, "and here is the latest talk, and you had better brace yourself for this. You know that they think that Carol is a cocaine dealer and that she is from a family of shrimp thieves." And you nod yes as Herb continues. "well, now they're saying that since you and Carol live together, then you must be a dealer too and a shrimp thief as well."

But for a long moment you can only look at Herb with dumbfounded surprise as your mouth opens and closes several times while you try to find words to say. And finally the only words that you can find to say are "ah, Jesus, Herb, you can't be serious." But right away Herb answers, "but I am serious, Ben, real serious, and the talk is serious, real serious."

So you shake your head in total disbelief at how things can become so distorted so quickly until they become one huge lie that is compounded on another huge lie that is compounded on yet another huge lie that are all automatically believed at the first telling without any opportunity for defense or explanation. And finally the only thing you can find to say is, "Herb, I told Carol one night at supper that I had heard that she was dealing cocaine. She stopped eating and she looked me straight in the eyes for a long time, then finally she said, Ben, I do not deal cocaine. Then after another long moment she said, now, you can either believe me or you can believe these worthless McIntosh County rednecks. Then we just looked at each other for another long moment without talking. Then we began to eat supper again, and finally we began to talk about other things."

And just as you are about to tell Herb that that is where things still stand between you and Carol, that she was right that you can either believe her or believe the rednecks, you see Jerry Harrelson large and lunging at your back in the mirror and right away you feel him grab your collar and jerk you backwards off the barstool.

And while you are in midair and about to sprawl across the floor that click happens again that so often happens to commercial fishermen always on boats and so close to constant sudden danger the click where afterwards time and people and events slow and slow until all things are now seen sharply individually and far more clearly and where all your senses are heightened and strengthened as your personal survival now becomes paramount and the placement and the movement of anything and all things are now graphically recorded and identified and scaled for most immediate threat while at the same time a corrective reaction is automatically formulated all in a single instant, so that if this happens you will do that to defend against it, and if that happens you will do this to defend against it, so that by the time you do sprawl across the floor you are already scrambling to get up on your hands and knees and then you are scrambling under a pool table and now you are standing up on the other side of the pool table. And as you come up to standing you grab a laying on the table pool stick by the small end and right away you already have the pool stick coming around fast with the big end coming first in a wide wide horizontal arc that makes a long whooooosh sound. And while the whooooosh continues whooooosh, drunk Jerry is straightening up from looking under the pool table to see where the hell you had gone. But the long whooooosh abruptly ends with a loud short whaaack to the side of Jerrys' head just as he has straightened. And in slow slow motion you see the red blood explode exploding from Jerrys' ear. And you see Jerrys' jaw suddenly zig zag sideways as it comes unhinged and becomes awfully distorted. And from Jerrys' now opening now gaping mouth comes a sound that sounds something like awwk just before there is a rush of foamy red spittle blood that now gushes. And without seeing them you instantly know that all the other rednecks are closing in. So with the two foot splintered small end of the pool stick still in your hand you start around the pool table for Jerry. And as you come around the table you see that Herb has Jerrys' drunk buddy by the throat with one of his big flat cast iron skillet oyster picking and clam digging hands, while his other big flat cast iron skillet oyster picking and clam digging hand is giving the guys' blue choked and red eyes popped face slow friendly love pats that have already ruined the guys' face forever. Now you are around the table and on your knees beside Jerry sprawled on the floor. Now you have the splintered small end raised high with both hands to bring it down hard and into Jerrys' chest deep. But suddenly you are knocked off your knees by the rush of rednecks and the splintered end goes rattling across the floor. Now you feel a fist opening the still sore welt on your forehead. Now you feel a boot stomping your still sore ribs. Now through the tangle of thrashing arms and legs you see a rush of Deputy Sheriff uniforms.

Now you and Herb are standing with your hands handcuffed in front of you in the middle of all the overturned bar stools at the bar. The ceiling lights are on and in this bare bulb glare you right away see how dirty and worn and paint flaked the Laughing Gull actually is. Deputies have the rednecks in a group over against the wall by the front door. The emergency medical people are very busy with Jerry and his buddy. They have Jerry on his side so he doesn't drown in his own spittle blood. There is already a good size pool of it around his head. And everytime Jerry makes that awwk sound the pool gets bigger and redder. The Head Deputy finishes his talk with the bartender down the bar and goes to talk with several mingling about Deputies. The group of rednecks have already been cleared out. The emergency medical people have already rolled Jerry and his buddy out on gurneys. But Jerrys' awwk pool still shines big and red in the glaring ceiling lights. Now the Head Deputy comes over and takes the handcuffs off you and Herb and says, "the bartender told me what happened so I can't hold you Carolina boys for anything." Then he pauses before saying, "but I would think long before coming back in here, and I would think hard about going on back to Carolina all together." Then another pause before saying, "have I made myself absolutely clear?"

CHAPTER TWELVE

Then in the night you are once again drifting helplessly on the part of the shrimp bin wall. And on one of his slow revolutions when you both are at the heights of your separate swells rise, Forrest sees your frantic waving, and he waves back frantically also. Then for a long time you all wave at each other on each of his slow revolutions in the big plastic deck cooler when your separate swells are at their height. Then suddenly as if by agreement you all stop waving. And now when the swells height and his revolutions meet, you all simply helplessly look at each other pitifully. Because the distance between you all continues to increase. Because gradually Forrest and the cooler have become smaller and smaller and smaller still. Until now, finally, you no longer can see them. And the sudden rush of terror and loneliness is staggering. So you wipe away the tears that have begun. And in this so real anguish you once again wake yourself. But Carol is not here in bed with you to hold you close and softly say it's all right Ben it's all right Ben.

So with the blanket from the bed you walk down the dark hall to the living room. And with a beer from the frig in the kitchen and your pack of cigarettes and lighter and ashtray now beside you on the couch you sit with the blanket pulled up and look out the living room window across the yard to the dirt road beyond. And in the dim darkness because of your neighbors' porch light you see and hear the slanted rain and you see and hear how much the wind is moving the live oaks and their Spanish moss. And you have been down here long enough now so you can project how rough the sounds are and farther out how rough the sea is by how much movement there is in the live oaks and their Spanish moss in your yard here back a hundred yards from the open marsh. And looking from your dark living room to the dim darkness in your yard you right away know how miserable it would be to be on a boat on the sounds tonight. And you right away know how truly miserable it would be to be on a boat on the sea tonight. So you sit safe and warm and dry on your couch looking out and you are glad that you and Mike decided not to go shrimp fishing in the morning.

Because when he pulled into your yard to drop you off after you all had had supper with Johanna, he shut off the engine and the lights of his truck and for a minute you all just sat there and saw and heard the hard blowing rain jarring his truck. Then after the minute Mike said, "so what do you think about in the morning?" So you said, "whatever you think, Mike, we've shrimped through worse." So you all sat without a decision for another minute. "I don't know, Ben, it'll be a couple of days before this mess blows itself out, why don't we give the shrimp a rest till then?" And right away you said, "that's fine with me, Mike, we've been pushing ourselves hard for months now." Then you added, "and Johanna gave us a lot to think about tonight." And Mike answered, "yes she did, Ben, so let's give the shrimp a rest till this mess blows itself out."

No one can beat Johanna at pot roast with carrots and potatoes and onions for its chomp chomp chomp good good good. So for awhile you and Mike stay very busy at putting a big dent in the now no longer piled high platter while Johanna smiles her approval. Then when you and Mike are finally full and smiling your approval also and sitting back in your chair she said, "okay, now let's get down to business, because you all deserve to know exactly where I stand. Forrest could have stopped all this trouble long before it got this bad. And while I've tried to do what I thought he would have done, I haven't been able to stop it. In fact, every week it seems to get worse. Ben, since you and Herb got into the fight at the Laughing Gull several weeks ago, the whole County has been in an uproar. But as Forrest said many times, 'Johanna our business is running a shrimp dock. What happens away from the dock is not our business!' There always is some kind of uproar going on in this County because that is the kind of place it is. The fight didn't have anything to do with the dock, so I've stayed out of it. Just as I've stayed out of all the talk about Carol. I knew the talk when you first asked me about her, Ben, but I didn't repeat it because, again, it didn't have anything to do with the dock. So you're on your own in deciding that one, Ben. Mike, the talk about you and Ben being boat sinkers is ridiculous and we three know it. But that does have everything to do with the dock, so I'm very much concerned about it. Several of the boat crews have told me to tell you all to dock Silly Sally somewhere else, or they will dock somewhere else. And this is my decision. For months now you all have been out shrimping every boat from Savannah to St. Mary's. And the dock has made thirty cents a pound from all that shrimp, and a lot more when I've been able to sell retail. So I'm not about to tell you all to dock somewhere else. If the other crews want to move their boats, fine, but you all are welcome at my dock for as long as you want to dock there. So that settles that."

Then Johanna paused and looked at you and Mike to be sure you understood the decision and that she would stick to it no matter what. And when you all nodded that you understood, she said, "now on a more personal note. Ben, you and Forrest fussed constantly about everything, but he thought, thinks, the world of you, and I do too. Mike, you drifted from boat to boat and couldn't seem to get serious about shrimp fishing until you and Ben got together on Silly Sally. I'm proud of you, and Forrest will be too when he gets back. So something good has come from losing Forrest and Mustang. But the winter storms have started and the hard freezes will start soon. So there is only a month or so of the cold water run left in this season. By mid January it will all be over with until spring. And when the season ends, then, we all hope, all the talk and trouble will end too." Then Johanna shrugs and opens her hands palms up on the table, and says, "so let's just keep doing what we have been doing, and let the rest just take care of itself."

Then Johanna's face brightened now that the formal dock owner business is done. But you noticed that the smile lines around her eyes that before had been simply that, smile lines, now have a weariness and a sadness and a responsibleness to them. Because single handedly managing a small business that grosses well into the several millions of dollars over a six month season period in a naturally chaotic world anyway that is still very much a mans' world of hard men long accustomed to dealing with only other hard men has brought its full price along with it. But her smile now was a happy smile in spite of all that, and you noticed that it is a proud smile and a relaxed smile as well, as she asked, "so what are you all going to do during the off season?" And right away you answered, "well Mike wants us to take Silly Sally around to the Gulf to Louisiana to shrimp until spring. And I would love to see that area, and how they shrimp there, especially their butterfly nets. But Herbs' oyster business is going from bad to worse real fast, so I may stay and help him." But right away Johanna added, "plus you don't want to leave Carol." So you blushed and said trailing off, "plus I don't want to leave Carol." Then Johanna said, "well, obviously, our plans to shrimp Mexico during the off season here ended when Forrest got lost. But that's probably just a pipe dream that we've had for all these years anyway."

But with this mention of lost Forrest, her smile suddenly left and her face suddenly stared. Then she said, "there is something else I have to tell you." And right away her eyes glistened and her bottom lip quivered. And right away you thought, 'oh shit, what's the bad news now?' Then Johanna touched her forehead with trembling fingers and said, "the phone was ringing when I got in from the dock last night. When I answered it a man started speaking Spanish real fast as though he couldn't stay on the phone long. I said what several times, and I tried to break in and say that I didn't speak Spanish, but he just kept talking real fast. I picked up a little Spanish when we shrimped Mexico, but that was a long time ago, and he had caught me by surprise, and he talked so fast I just couldn't understand anything he said. Then he quickly hung up." Then Johannas' face drained of color. Then she said, "but twice during what he said he very distinctly said, 'Forrest Sawyer!" And right away you saw that Mikes' mouth had suddenly opened and that his face had suddenly drained. So you knew that your mouth had opened and that your face had drained also.

Then the stunned silence just went on and on until it became huge. And all that you all could do was to sit and look at each other in stunned shock. Then Johanna reached across and took your hand with one of her hands, and she reached across and took Mikes' hand with her other hand, and she said, "he called to tell me something very important about Forrest, but I don't know what it was."

And remembering all this now you pull the blanket up closer because the hair on your back neck tingles and a shiver shutter runs along your shoulders. So you sit on the couch in the dark living room and you look across the yard through the slanted rain and the blowing live oaks and you hope upon hope for the very best for Forrest, but it does not look good for Forrest wherever he is and however he is and whatever has happened to him. So you shake your head sadly and you clinch your teeth grimly for Forrest, but you know that he can endure a great deal just as all commercial fishermen can endure a great deal and do.

Then you see the light come on in the bedroom of your neighbor across the dirtroad so you know that it is just after three o'clock and that he is getting up to get ready to go work his line of crab traps blowing mess or no blowing mess not so much for crabs but to try and keep his traps in the lee of the marsh islands and in deep water because this blowing mess can easily roll and tumble and crush his ten thousand dollars worth of wire crab traps if they are left exposed in open waters for too long. And you remember that bay fishermen in open skiffs take daily and constant punishment also, and that they must be just as hard as the hardest men aboard trawlers. So you remember the stories that you had heard back home about the commercial clammers from Swansboro which is a fishing village down south and west of your home in Atlantic. How at different times of the year they would haul their skiffs and travel coastal North Carolina in search of concentrations of clams. And how the local clammers hated and feared and respected them. And how news of their arrival in an area spread like wild fire and with the dread of a plague of locust, until their reputation had become almost mystical. Then one morning during about as bad a blow as you remember Atlantic having, when Core Sound looked like an angry sea fighting itself, and all the local shrimpers and crabbers and clammers and gillnetters had decided to stay tied to the dock and give their whichever fishery a rest for the day at least, there four of the Swansboro clammers were nonchalantly launching their skiffs down at the marina. They had suddenly just appeared like the loudest clap of lightening there ever had been. First one skiff was launched, then a second skiff was launched. Then the two guys to a skiff started transferring their gear from their trucks to their skiffs. Well, most of the fishermen of Atlantic were watching them with dreadful awe from closed windows from cracked doors from behind whatever from a distance. And you remember looking from the awe staring towns' fishermen to the four guys who looked about as ordinary as all fishermen look ordinary and wondering how and why these four ordinary looking guys could strike such fear in the hearts of so many other fishermen.

So you walked down to them and said good morning and they looked at you and right away recognized you as a fisherman so they said good morning back. Then you asked if they needed help in loading their skiffs but right away they said nope we can handle it in a way that quickly ended that. But their skiffs were just the ordinary long wide flat bottom well skiffs that most bay fishermen use who often work shallow water. But their skiffs did have a sturdily worn look about them that somehow set them apart. And their gear was the usual assortment of rakes and hacks and buckets and tubs that most clammers use. But their gear had that same sturdily worn look also. Then you noticed that the four guys had that same sturdily worn look. The same look that is so difficult to describe that you see on a few fishermen in a crowd of fishermen. Then after the abrupt silence that followed nope we can handle it you looked out across Core Sound and said she's blowing about as bad as I remember seeing her. So the four of them followed your look across the calm inside the marina to the fighting herself angry Core Sound and they said at the same time yeah she's blowing pretty good. Then when they were ready they just got into their skiffs and ran right out into the very worst of it as though Core Sound were slick calm flat and resting. And you remember standing there thinking those fuckers are hungry and those fuckers are salty and those fuckers know what the hell they're doing.

And sure enough that afternoon they ran back into the calm of the marina with that same sturdily worn look of just another workday on the water. But they sold more clams to the buyer that afternoon than all the local clammers had sold to him in a month. Then they just hauled their skiffs and just suddenly disappeared ahead of the same loudest lightening clap there had ever been. And you remember thinking I don't know how those fuckers did it but those hungry salty fuckers do know what they're doing yes hell they do. Then you thought well our clammers can forget about going clamming for a good long while and I mean a good long while, because those fuckers got them all.

So you sit here in the dark of your living room and you smile to yourself as you remember and you look across your yard at the blowing mess that is still there. And right away you realize that for the past months you and Mike and Silly Sally as well have had that same sturdily worn look that a few fishermen have in a crowd of fishermen.

But your eyes are closing more often now. And each time they are staying closed for longer now. So you do not need another beer to get back to sleep. So you settle farther on the couch and you bring the blanket closer warmer. But car lights out on the dirtroad seem as if they are about to turn into your yard so you raise up looking hoping. But the car lights continue along and then go on by so you settle back down because it is not Carol coming home. And with sleep nearer closer now you wonder where Carol is and why she is not here with you where she should be. But right away you realize that this is not fair because during the past months there have been many nights when Carol was here alone waiting for you. But you and Mike had anchored Silly Sally behind Sapelo Island or behind St. Catherines' Island or behind another barrier island to save the wear and the tear and the fuel of a long run in and then a long run from the dock. That or else you came home exhausted for a late supper and a quick shower and then several hours of sleep before returning to the dock. And we are always more aware when others are not there when we need them than when we are not there when others need us. So not being there for the other has been about equal between you and Carol for the past months.

But it is the vague explanations or the no explanations of where she goes and what she does that bother you the most. Because the selling of shore bird sketches to tourists at the pier at St. Simons and the taking care of her Dad in Brunswick simply cannot account for her frequent and long absences. And several times you have decided to follow her so you will finally know where she really goes and what she really does. But however innocently and out of curiosity that following her might begin, it would end in sneaking among lies and stalking among distrust. And you do not want to become a sneaker and a stalker. Because you have always been proud of being too open and too direct even though they often get you into trouble. So it comes back to what it has always come back to. That you can believe Carol, or you can not believe Carol. It is as simple as that. But your head has already decided that Carol is dealing. But your dick really does not give a damn. Because a stiff dick does not have a conscious.

CHAPTER THIRTEEN

The living area of his trawler is more home to a fisherman than any land home could ever be. It is the smell of last summers sweat and last months spoiled milk and last weeks spilled grease and last nights juicy fart, all together in a lingering bouquet. It is the seawater saltiness that crusts everything. It is the brown limpness of the bunk sheets that can never again become white and crisp. It is the lumpy sag of the mattress that always brings instant sleep. It is the assbone jarring hardness of the booth seat at the worn smooth and carved on eating table. It is the huge assortment of one of a kind glasses and plates and bowls and knives and forks and spoons that are gathered over much time and from a hundred places. It is standing in the center and damn near being able to touch booth and frig and sink and counter and stove and table and racks and shelves and cabinets. Whatever you want, whatever you need, all within an arms reach. And it cheerfully welcomes you at the end of a long hard day. And it grudgingly sends you out on your grumbling way before dawn. Yes, it is more home to a fisherman than any land home could ever be.

So here you and Mike and Petey too are cozy and warm inside Silly Sally and anchored for the night in the mouth of the South Newport River in the lee of the cold wind that is blowing across St. Catherines' Island from the sea. With Petey at Mikes' feet gnawing contentedly on a ham bone. With you and Mike hunched over big and I mean big bowls of ham hocks and black-eyes at the so familiar table. With a platter of slow fried thin and crunchy cornbread between you. But before you ladle the ham hocks and black-eyes into your bowls, you dump diced tomato and diced onion into your bowls. Then you dump three dripping full ladles of ham hocks and black-eyes into you bowls. Then you and Mike grab a big mixing spoon with one hand and grab a piece of crunchy thin cornbread with the other hand. Now it is every man for himself and Katie bar the door and damn the torpedoes and all that stuff. Yeah man!

Now you shift your assbone on the hard seat to find a more comfortable position and you take a drink of iced tea from your glass and you knock the cigarette ash into your empty bowl and you continue, "the man has a hell of a business plan, Mike, and he can quickly tell you more about oysters and clams than you ever really wanted to know. Herbs' a hell of a shellfish fisherman, Mike, and he really does know what he is doing. But as hard as he has worked the past three years, everything he has tried has failed. Not completely, but just enough so it isn't quite profitable or it really isn't worth the effort for the small profit. It's uncanny, Mike, it's as though Herb is doomed to fail no matter what he does."

And right away Mike answers, "he is, Ben! Hell, you've been down here long enough so you should realize that. And Herb certainly should have realized that long ago. These people do not want an outsider to come here and build a successful shellfish business. Therefore, Herb will not build a successful shellfish business. It's that simple. And it's that obvious." And then Mike spreads his hands palms up to emphasize that point.

But right away you answer with just as much emphasis, "but Mike, if Herb could get the wild harvesting profitable, then he could build a shucking house. And when that is profitable, then he could build a clam and oyster spawning and outgrown farm. And when that is profitable, then he could build a steamed shellfish restaurant out on I-95. See, the man really does have a hell of a business plan. And combined, the business would mean thirty or forty pretty good paying year round jobs. And as poor as McIntosh County is, that would help a lot. Mike, you know that shellfish farms and shrimp farms and fish farms are the future. Well, Herb is just trying to be a part of it."

But Mike just shakes his head no, and says, "none of that matters, Ben, it doesn't. The only thing that matters is what Herb did by coming down here." And you start to say but, but Mike holds up his hand whoa and says, "let me finish. Ben, the clams and oysters here have always been what the crabbers and the shrimpers got by on during January, February and March when there weren't any crabs and shrimp. We, and I say we because I did it too, we all did, we harvested them and sold them wherever we could and for whatever we could get. There wasn't any such thing as shellfish leases with exclusive harvesting rights. True we ignored the rules and regulations for proper refrigeration and clean handling. But McIntosh County had always been the bootleg capital of coastal Georgia. And, yes, we were bootleggers, but we got through the winter. And that's all we were trying to do, survive until spring, until the crab and shrimp season began again. But all that suddenly changed when Herb came. I mean the whole County was in an uproar. Herb was resented and even hated. And he still is today. These people don't care anything about business plans and shellfish farms and year round jobs. They just want things back the way they were, back the way things had always been. When Herb hires them to dig clams or to pick oysters, they only bring him half of what they harvest. They hide the other half and go back later and get it and sell it through the usual bootleg channels. They are going to break Herb, if they haven't already, and that's all they care about."

So for a long minute there is only silence between you all sitting at the dish cluttered table with Petey gently snoring there at Mikes' feet with the outside cold wind gently rocking warmly lighted Silly Sally snugly at anchor. Then, finally, you say, "well, that's the most ignorant and short sighted thinking that I've ever heard of." But Mike only shrugs resigned and says, "Ben, there's no way in hell that Herb is going to build a successful shellfish business down here." And that ended that conversation.

Then in the night there is the hiss of the propane heater that is tucked down in the corner out of the way. And there is the dimness of the night light that just does open the darkness. And in the bunk above you hear Mike shift his position in the sag of his bunk and when he does then Petey shifts his position there asleep at Mikes' feet. And you know that you were awakened to half asleep when Silly Sally lost the strain on the anchor line from the incoming tide. Now in your mind you can see her beginning to drift and beginning to meander in the now idle high water slack. And from above you can see her white boat outline in the cold star light against the black water. There are her red and green running lights on. There is her tall white at anchor light on. And there just upriver is the Wave Dancer quietly at anchor also. And there just up river from her the Miss Catherine is quietly at anchor also. Three mighty fishing vessels at rest for now from the sea. Six mighty commercial fishermen at rest for now from the sea. Now in your half asleepness you feel Silly Sally take a good strain against the anchor line having already swung full about in the now outgoing tide. So all is well in your world. So all is right in your world. So you snuggle deeper into the sag of your warm bunk.

The first collision caused the damage. The second collision caused Mike and me to not be able to stop further damage while it could still be stopped. Because Wave Dancer slipped her anchor when the outgoing tide reached its point of relentless serge. But her anchor had good purchase during the relentless serge of the incoming tide. But now in the relentless serge of the outgoing tide and in the soft bottom that is below there, it simply lost its purchase. And that is all that it takes, a momentary loss of purchase, and in soft bottom the purchase cannot be gained again. Because the anchor just begins to slide along and there is not anything quick and fast in its way to snag it to catch it to grab it to hold it. So now it just continued to slide along the soft bottom so smoothly that neither Andy or Bill there asleep aboard Wave Dancer felt the bounce and the tumble of the anchor along the anchor chain that they would have felt had it been sliding along hard bottom. So they slept on peacefully even though Wave Dancer was swinging broadside now in the surging tide because of the swirls and the eddies that are within the tide.

So Wave Dancer collided with Silly Sally late in the cold night starry darkness, and the damage was already done before Mike and me could stop it from becoming fatal. The first collision was when Wave Dancers' right side at her wheelhouse gave Silly Sallys' bow an off angle blow that was heavy enough so our anchor lost its purchase also, and right away she began to swing broadside in reaction to this heavy blow. And the second collision was immediately after the first collision when Wave Dancers' big stern came big swinging around and crashed into our midships at our living quarters. And the only thing that is worse than collision at sea, is fire at sea. Just the thought of fire onboard their trawler scares the bejesus shit out of commercial fishermen. It truly does.

You do not get use to crisis at sea. Not ever. Because each crisis at sea is new and it is different and it is separate. And each crisis at sea has its own terror that afterwards is special to only it. So the loss of Mustang when you and Forrest were run over by the freighter has one distinct terror for you. And now the burning of Silly Sally to the waterline will have another distinct terror for you. But you do get use to automatically letting your at sea survival instincts to take over for your land problem solving techniques. Because fishermen must have quick and correct instinct reactions to crisis, or they will not be fishermen for very long. Reacting quickly can be learned with practice. But reacting correctly can only be inherited. You either have that, or else you do not have that.

The deep sags of our bunk mattresses keep Mike and me from being thrown out of our bunks during the first collision crash of violence and noise. But asleep at Mikes' feet, Petey is on a level and right away he is thrown out and across and he hits the cabinets with his head way too hard and the sound of his neck cracking is loud and the sound of his yelp is soft and he is dead when he hits the deck with a thud and a tumble. And you hear Mike yell Petey and you hear feel Mike frantically scrambling to get out of his bunk. And you hear yourself yell what the hell and you feel Silly Sally lurch harshly and then keel over and then right away right herself and you feel the anchor suddenly lose its purchase. And right away everything is flying across everywhere as pots and cans and dishes and everything are slamming across your bunk like fired missiles. And you hear Mike yell Petey again and you see his feet coming out and down from his bunk. And right away you know that you must get forward and get the lights on and get the engine cranked and get the bilge on. But everything keeps flying across at you and hitting you and hurting you and you cannot get your getting out of the goddamn bunk coordinated.

Then everywhere around you see the brilliant flash of the

gas heater being suddenly thrown forward and then suddenly snatched back by the copper tubing that goes under the sink and then outside to the big cylinder. Then there is the hiss of the escaping gas where the bend in the tubing tears. Then there is the explosion of the heater igniting the escaping gas. And right away you know that you must get outside and turn off the gas at the big cylinder. Because the lighting and the cranking and the bilging of Silly Sally can sure as hell wait now.

But now there is the heat and the flames and the smoke that are everywhere all around in here now. And you hear Mike yell Ben and you hear you yell yeah. But now only seconds after the first collision crash comes the second collision crash of equal violence and noise. And something hits you really hard wham and your hands and your arms are outstretched trying to find something anything to hold on to and you do not know whether you are up or you are down and you feel as though you are going to throw up. But all of a sudden Mikes' heavy weight comes slamming down on top of you and then you are on top of dead Petey. And now you look at the blowtorch flames that is the torn copper tubing and then you smell your hair burning and Peteys' hair burning and Mikes' hair burning. And right away you know that there is no way in hell that you can get outside and turn off the gas at the big cylinder in time.

But right away, too, you feel Mike being grabbed from on top of you. Then you feel yourself being grabbed from on top of dead Petey. Then you see hands reaching beyond you and grabbing

132

pulling dead Petey outside also. Now you all are out in the cold starry darkness that feels so very wonderful. Now a face is in your face and the face is yelling are you allright are you allright? But you yell at the face gas cylinder gas cylinder gas cylinder until the face disappears. But it burns to breathe. But you feel the seawater wetness of the deck that is so very wonderful also. But in the starry darkness you feel something spewing from your mouth, and right away you know that it is ham hocks and black-eye peas and so forth.

CHAPTER FOURTEEN

There is good stubble now where your eyelashes and your eyebrows and your hair had been. So at least there is that on the return to your looking normal again. But people still stare even though baldness is common. Because no eyelashes and no eyebrows in addition to baldness is not common. And so they still stare as though you are a freak. But there is good stubble now and this will quickly lengthen and it will thicken. And you have finally peeled as many layers of scorched skin from your face and from your hands as you will peel. But it will be months before the peeled splotches soften and before they fade.

But you are shaving once again, if very tenderly, and this helps how you feel about yourself. Because you have never felt comfortable whenever you have not shaved every morning. But today you wait to shave until now just before time to go to Johannas' for her Christmas party so at least the fresh shave will look good because there is not a damn thing that you can do about the mess that your face looks like. So you put the razor down on the sink and you rinse off the remaining soap and you gently dab your face with the towel and you look closer in the mirror and you think what a hell of a mess my face is, what a hell of a mess my face has become since I came down here last spring only since then. But I really do not want to go to Johannas' party because people will stare and they will talk behind my back and they will snicker that the son of a bitch got what he deserved and it should have been worse if you ask me. But since Forrest has been lost at sea Johanna and me want to be with each other not all of the time but some of the time because we share something with each other that we do not share with other people and we cannot share with other people. So I have to go to the party tonight. But I really do not want to go to the party tonight. But I do want to be around where Johanna is for a while at least. And besides, Georgia McIntosh will be there.

But your Mom is going to throw a damn fit when she sees the mess that your face has become when you go home next week for the several days of Christmas. And I mean a sure enough real damn fit for fair thee well with hot tears and anquish gasps and hand wringing too as well as hands to her face in disbelief in oh my god shock of look what the sea that she has done to my precious boy and because why? Because the sea that she has no call no good reason to cause all of this destruction to you personally to you privately especially because you have not will not refuse her by throwing down your fishing boots and walking inland in dismissal of her and thereby turning your back on her ultimately in denying her in simply ignoring her completely. And I absolutely will not allow her that, her to cause this to happen to you again, no I will not, no not again. And so your Mom will embrace you and hug you close to her warm breast too closely even so that sheltered so no further destruction can possibly happen to you personally to you privately.

And now knowing exactly how her too close embrace hug breast will feel and now looking in the mirror at your face mess there suddenly is the boyhood memory before you in the night when from their bedroom down the hall there is her insistent hushed voice saying no dad no dad not tonight because she did not want to tonight but he had to tonight and so he just went ahead and did and now looking closely in the mirror you still remember the anger at him that became the rage at him that became the jealousy of him as you lay in your boyhood bed and did nothing.

But you had forgotten how good it is to be in a crowd of people who all like each other and who all enjoy being with each other. Because people become too busy and too distracted and therefore too separated from others. So tonight Johannas' Christmas party is going very well indeed. And the people are trying especially hard to enjoy each other even more because Forrests' absence leaves a huge void that everyone is trying especially hard to not notice. Because these are the people who grew up with Forrest and Johanna and therefore are the people who know them better than anyone. So Forrests' absence only makes them laugh a little louder and makes them smile a little bigger to prove that they are not noticing Forrests' absence. And Johanna is especially gay and especially talkative tonight as well. She is out doing herself as she fusses and hovers about the buffet table to ensure that everyone fills their plates with all the many different foods that they could ever want. And the people are saying in whispers among themselves how well Johanna is handling Forrests' being lost at sea as many commercial fishermen down through the years have become lost at sea. Because after the first month of being shy and unsure of herself, didn't she take a firm grip of the shrimp dock business and begin to run it with the assurance of a man? And isn't she shoving and tossing one hundred pound boxes of iced shrimp about with the best of them? And doesn't she handle the never ending boat crew disputes quickly and fairly and finally? And doesn't she handle the complicated shrimp price fluctuations with the wholesalers and the retailers and the distributors with shrewdness and with cold calculation? So, yes, everyone whispers among themselves that Johanna is also handling Forrests' being lost at sea very well indeed.

So you do everything you can to be sure that the ice bucket is refilled and that more tea is brought and that another bowl of potato salad is brought and that another plate of sliced ham is brought and that the empty bowls and plates are returned to the kitchen. Because you and Johanna share something that the others do not share and cannot share. And tonight is really very much Johannas' night and you want it to be her best night in a very long time because she deserves it. So you move among the crowd as quietly as you possibly can as you go about doing the things that you hope will please Johanna.

But these people do not know why you of all people are here at her party in the first place. Because you did not grow up with any of them. Because you are not even from around here.

Because you are only a striker on a shrimp boat sterndeck and strikers come a dime a dozen cheap. Because you have the vivid physical scars of why commercial fishing is by far the most dangerous profession of all professions ever. And these people tonight do not want you here as a vivid reminder of that constant fact. So you stay busy in the background and you do not draw anymore attention to yourself than is necessary. But during your trips to and from the kitchen, when you look out at the happy crowd that is mingling and is shifting and is mingling again in ones and twos and threes and fours about the living room and on into the den and out into the large glassed patio, there is Georgia McIntosh herself for sure and at long last. And she is as blonde beautiful as she always is in your dreams. And she terrifies you. Because you have not forgotten how simply she dismissed you as not even worth recognition at the pool table at the Laughing Gull that night so many months ago.

And when you close the refrigerator door and turn, Georgia McIntosh is so close before you that the movement of your turning is enough to move the fine blonde hair that surrounds her face. So close that the effect of her perfume is full. And you can see the delicate line of her eye liner. And you can see the exact smear of her eye shadow. And you can see the perfect outline of her lipstick. And you can see the tiny pores in her pale skin. But before you can pull back and say excuse me she says you aren't very bright are you and before you can say what she says you just don't get it do you? And in your confusion now she says why don't you haul your sorry ass back to North Carolina or wherever the hell it is that you are from because all you've done down here is bring us grief and we don't want any more of your damn grief. And just as suddenly now she turns and walks away and then out of the kitchen.

And when you find Georgia in the den and separated enough from the others you go to her and you say look let's talk Georgia let me explain. But right away she says I don't know what you're talking about. And as you quickly try to think of a way to simply say that you are really just a good guy who is hard working and who loves being a fisherman and who is doing the best he can and can't we be friendly and talk some and maybe spend time together and get to know each other, Georgia abruptly turns and walks away again.

But her father and her grandfather and her great grandfather were lifetime commercial fishermen, as were yours also, so you do not understand how she cannot understand that you are just the next generation of that long proud tradition whether fishing North Carolina or Georgia or Louisiana or Alaska doesn't matter. So you walk after Georgia. But she knows you are so right away she stops and she turns and she holds out her hand palm out in stop do not follow me do not stalk me. So you stop and you put out your hands down and palms up in please I am not going to hurt you I just want us to talk to get to know each other because I really am just a hard working nice guy fisherman. So for several seconds with her hand still out in stop she simply looks at you while she decides. And she is so beautiful that you no longer can speak nor can you breathe.

139

Now she lowers her stop hand and she reaches and she takes one of your hands with her hand. Now she is leading you by the hand out into the glassed patio and to a corner where the others are not.

And now in the corner she turns to you and her hand lets go of your hand and her hand slowly comes up to your face and then her fingers very gently touch the ridged welt that came when Forrest and Mustang became lost at sea and then her fingers very tenderly touch the burn splouches that came when Silly Sally became burned to the waterline. And now she takes aside her hand and now her hand suddenly gives the side of your face a sharp short stinging slap. Slap! And now as you startle in surprise and in pain, she moves much closer and now her face once again is very close to your face and right away you see that her beautiful soft face has become contorted and that her beautiful soft face has become ugly. And now so close to your face that her too close face has began to blur she says in a harsh spitting whisper I'm going to say this simply so even dumbass you can understand it. Harsh spitting whisper saying there will be a day when there will be no commercial fishermen on any ocean on any waters, anywhere, and we will see to that that we promise, and when that happens and it will happen soon because it has already begun, all of you will be as dead and lifeless as the washed up marshwrack. And then just as sudden as the sudden slap she steps aside and she walks away and you are left alone with your startled face your stinging face. But it is awhile before you leave the corner.

But the good good party does wonders for Johannas'

laughter for Johannas' beaming smile. And you are glad for her and you are proud of her even when she becomes giggly from too much wine. Because fun tonight has been long in coming for her and she deserves tonight and she needs tonight after all of these months of sadness of worry of work. So you are busy in the kitchen washing things and drying things and putting things away while Johanna gayly says good night to the last of the people at the front door. Now she comes to you and she gives you a quick hug and then she does a little whirl to over by the sink and she gayly says wasn't tonight fun Ben wasn't tonight such good good fun did you have fun Ben and you smile yes and you nod yes and you say yes that you had fun saying yes to not spoil it for her sake at least and she throws out her arms and she says oh I had such good fun tonight, Ben, but I couldn't have without you Ben because you were everywhere doing everything so thank you Ben for being here tonight for letting me have tonight and you blush and you shrug ah shucks ma'am twern't nothing really like that as Johanna stands by the sink gayly and just beaming her beaming smile.

But you do not know who makes the first movement. All you know is that suddenly Johanna is full length pressed in your arms and that you are kissing her reaching up mouth first hard then soft then hard again. And her mouth is kissing your mouth back first hard then soft then hard again. And her mouth is wet. And her mouth is urgent also. Then suddenly again she quickly strongly pushes herself away to arms length from you and there is the look of surprise on her face and she says no, Ben, no, we can't, you

141

know we can't. You know we mustn't. And you say yes I know we can't we mustn't. And you say I'm sorry, Johanna, I didn't know that was going to happen, I didn't mean for that to happen. But you stop before you say that you didn't want that to happen. So Johanna stands there with her outstretched hands at arms length gripping your arms to keep you strongly pushed away to arms length as you both try to not breathe so loud.

Then you watch as the look on Johannas' face goes from surprise to concern. But then the look on her face becomes what urgent looks like. And now her face begins to flush with red. And now her eyes begin to brighten. And with her loud breathing Johanna hoarsely whispers Ben we can't make love you know we can't make love and you know why. And you say yes I know we can't make love and I know why. But you feel the flushing with red beginning on your face as well. And you feel your eyes brightening. Now the look of urgency on Johannas' face becomes really urgent. Now hoarsely again she whispers Ben we won't make love, but would you please would you please, please would you Ben? But you do not know what she wants you to please Ben do. So Johanna leads you by the arms to the kitchen table and she pulls out a chair and she turns it out and she takes you by the arms and she sits you in the chair.

And for several seconds she just stands before you with the look of really flushed urgency on her face, then she quickly pulls her loose blouse up and out from her loose skirt. Then her trembling fingers have her blouse unbuttoned and open wide.

Because the clothes she always wears are loose you did not know how full her breasts are. Now you know how full Johannas' breasts are. Now you know how large the brown around her nipples are. Now you know how long and firm her nipples are. Now Johanna hoarsely whispers please Ben please Ben. Now she brings her hands up and she puts them on either side of your head while one of her legs parts your legs way apart so she can stand in close between them. And sitting in the chair Johannas' breasts are at the same level with your face. And again she hoarsely whispers please Ben please Ben as she comes in closer. And her breasts become larger as they become closer. But it is how long and firm her coming closer nipples are that you see the most.

And with Johanna very close in between your legs now and with her hands on either side of your head she guides her right breast to your mouth and then she pushes her long firm nipple into your mouth. And Johanna says hhhhhh. And you feel her long firm nipple big in your mouth. And Johanna says hhhhhh. Then with her hands on either side of your head she pushes and pulls her long firm big nipple in short strokes in and out of your mouth. And Johanna says hhhhhh. But it is difficult for you to breathe with her full breast pressed so close around your face.

Now with even more urgency Johanna takes one of her hands away from you head, and then her hand is blindly searching frantically for one of your hands. And when her hand finds one of your hands her fingers quickly fold closed all of the fingers of your hand except the first two. Now her hand quickly takes your hand down and under and inside of her loose skirt, and bringing the skirt up as her hand brings your hand with your two fingers extended up and you feel her hand using your two fingers to move aside her panties. Now you feel your two fingers going all the way inside of Johanna. And now she really says hhhhhh. But it is still difficult for you to breathe with her long firm big nipple pushed into your mouth and her full breast pressed so close all around your face. Now Johanna begins to quiver. Now Johanna begins to jerk. Now you feel a gush of wet run over and down your hand that is being held strongly in place by her hand. And now you hear the wet dropping in drops on the floor between your legs.

Now her jerking begins to ease. Now her quivering begins to ease. Now her hand pulls your two fingers from inside of her and she brings your drenched hand from under her skirt. And when she pulls her long firm big nipple from your mouth you can breathe again. And right away Johanna begins to plead saying Ben don't tell anyone about this Ben please don't tell, this is just between us okay, no one else needs to know but us okay, promise me you won't tell please Ben but you have to go now because my neighbors will talk if you stay too long after the party so you have to go now okay but please don't tell this is just between us no one else needs to know okay Ben? Now she has you at the kitchen door. Now she has you outside on the back porch. And Johanna says promise me you won't tell Ben this is just between us Ben okay? Then she says good night Ben and thanks for tonight Ben. And right away she is back inside and she closes the door. So now you are standing outside alone in the dark night with your drenched wet hand and your hard dick that is cramped painfully inside your jeans. And you think maybe I can get home to the bathroom sink before my hand dries and I lose this hard.

CHAPTER FIFTEEN

You have not seen Mike since you have been back from home for Christmas. So when you meet him in his truck on the road you put up your hand in a big hello wave. But Mike cups his hand in his windshield as though he is holding a can of beer and he tilts it toward his mouth as though he is drinking the beer, then he points in the direction that the Laughing Gull is. So you nod yes and you give him a thumbs up in your windshield as you all go by each other. Then you pull into the next driveway and you back your truck around and you follow Mike.

And as soon as you sit beside Mike at the bar, the bartender recognizes you and right away he begins to shift his weight from one leg to the other leg and he begins to fold and refold a bar rag as he nervously decides whether to serve you or not. And in the mirror you see that the guys playing pool behind you are looking at you and they are talking among themselves as they nervously decide whether to stay or not. And when the bartender brings the beers for you and Mike you see him start to give you a stern warning. Then you see him decide that it is probably better to just let that sleeping dog lie.

So Mike says, "good to see you, Ben, long time no see," as you all shake hands firmly.

And you say, "yeah, what a month or so?" and right away in

your minds you both are onboard Silly Sally as she burns to the waterline and all of the terror that that included and all of the horror that followed that.

But Mike continues in spite of what he is reliving in his mind because life goes on and time heals all wounds, or those are the two favorite bullshit balm things that people like to say after personal tragedy, as he says, "yeah, a month or so at least."

So you say, "yeah, at least that," but by now it sounds awkward. Because it is awkward when you have lived and worked and ate and slept with someone onboard a trawler day and night week after week for so many months, then abruptly after the terror and the horror of a single night, you both simply go your separate ways without saying goodbye or even looking back.

So you both light cigarettes. So you both take drinks of your beers. So you both shift uneasily on your barstools. Because fishermen do not readily explain or justify or defend, anything. And when his still hurting has receded far enough, Mike says, "Petey was my heart, Ben. I just couldn't stay here with him gone. So I left the next morning after burying him. I should have told you I was going. And I should have told Don Arbo about Silly Sally burning. But getting in my truck and getting away from here fast was as much as I could handle at the time."

"I understand, Mike. And I understood then. And I wasn't dealing with things very well either. After losing Silly Sally after losing Mustang, I just shut my door to everything and everyone for a week. But I did call Don first. And he took it pretty well. At least after he got the hollering and the cussing over with. Silly Sally wasn't insured. So Don took a big loss."

"Yeah, I called the next week from Marathon, Florida, to see if he would help me get on a boat out of there. And he did. But by then he had accepted the loss of Silly Sally as just more of the risks of shrimp fishing. And I've accepted my losses as just more of the risks of shrimp fishing also. But it hasn't been easy. And it still isn't easy." Then Mike motions to the bartender for two more beers. And then he takes a deep breath and now you can see him forcing his face to brighten. "But I'm on Midnight Moon now, and I just came up for the rest of my stuff. We're pink shrimp fishing from the Keys down to Venezuela. A whole lot of open ocean, Ben, a whole lot of open ocean. It isn't anything like coastal shrimping around here."

"Whoa, that's bandido country."

And Mike laughs and says, "yeah, and smuggling too. Bullet boats crisscross and zoom everywhere, mostly heading north. DEA spotter aircraft crisscrossing high above. It's a real circus that's for sure. And there we are in the middle of all this nonchalantly trawling for pinks. Watching smugglers is entertainment, but watching for bandidos we take very seriously. None of us want to be captured and taken slave like Forrest."

"You think that's what happened to him?"

"That's the only thing I can figure, Ben."

"Yeah, maybe you're right. That makes as much sense as anything else. But poor Forrest."

"Poor Forrest is right." Then you both are quiet as you both try not to picture Forrest wherever he is whatever he is doing. Then you see Mike forcing his face to brighten again. "But Ben, you've never seen shrimp the size of these pinks. I mean they're damn near as big as bananas, I mean it."

So you say damn!

And Mike says, "really Ben, I mean it, I ain't kidding."

So you say damn! again.

And Mike says, "Ben, we're getting nine to ten dollars a pound at the dock, that's how big they are."

So now you say a really strong damn! to that.

And Mike says, "course I've only made one trip so far. But we caught forty boxes and that's damn near forty thousand dollars. Course the trip was a week and we burned a lot of fuel and we used tons of ice."

So right away you get the same visions of riches that you got when Forrest and Johanna were talking about shrimping the Gulf of Mexico when you first came down here so long ago it seems now.

"Course there are bandidos around, and we stay armed all of the time, and we take turns at sentry. Because shrimp that big are gold, Ben."

And as drastic as these changes would be in the boat living and the boat working routine, they seem a small price to pay an easy inconvenience to endure when compared to the visions of riches that you see as possible. Because there is the dreamer aspect of the ruby prospector the gold panner the diamond digger

149

in all commercial fishermen.   Because during the endless monotonous days of repetitive manual labor to just catch enough in whichever fishery to just pay the bills to just make a living, there is always the possibility of for once being at the right place at the right time when whatever you are fishing for has schooled in huge shoals has schooled in gigantic rafts and are just waiting there for you to come harvest them for you to damn near sink the boat bringing them aboard. But you remember what Herb said about the political pull the big time political clout that Forrest and Johanna tried so to buy year after year so they could once again shrimp the Gulf of Mexico that they had lucked into once years before but never could quite get again because since then they had simply become too politically insignificant in the global scheme of things to ever really get again if they ever had been politically significant to begin with which they never had been. So you ask Mike who owns Midnight Moon.

"Don't know.   No one on the boat knows.   The Captain doesn't even know.   The dock owner gives the Captain the boat share.   Then the dock owner deposits the rest in the Bank in the account of something named the Trans Ocean Trading Company. Probably an international conglomerate of some kind. Probably the Japanese. Or the Taiwanese. Who knows. But whoever they are they have a fleet of boats fishing out of Marathon. So they're big in fishing all right." Then you see Mikes' face brighten again. "Hey Ben, I can get you on a boat. Not my boat right now, but another boat. Then later we can get on a boat together, and it will be like it was on Silly Sally."

So right away you see yourself outbound on a sleek trawler and passing the Dry Tortugas on a calm sea in a warm wind under a brilliant sun. And the mirrored sunglasses make you mysterious and the deep tan makes you handsome and the holstered pistol makes you deadly. But right away, also, you see your Dads' fisherman weathered face the day after Christmas while you were just home as he quietly scolded you in the gentle way that he has of firmly reining in a wandering son, saying, son, you don't have any call to still be down there in that damn place getting yourself all wrecked up and scarred up until your Mom is about to worry herself sick with worry when the family needs you here because Tommy and me can't do it all and it is dumb to hire crew when that is what the younger son does like it or not want to or not until I step ashore which I am having to do more and more and then you will Captain the Betty Fagan. Because it is as though your Uncle Pharoah Farrow has been shot out of a cannon with the dock and the seafood buying business at Sealevel already up and running and I can't be on a boat and watching him at the same time, especially now that he is all fired up about our buying your friend Herbs' oysters and clams to sell to steam bars up here on top of the everything else that he has us over extended on. Course that will bail your friend Herb out of sure failure and bankruptcy, and I know that you want to help him in any way you can and have already, and maybe we can make a decent profit too from the arrangement if I can keep your Uncle Pharoah Farrow from promising everyone everything before we are even half way set up to deliver what he has already promised which is too much.

Saying, so son maybe the best thing would be for you to go ahead and stay on down there for a few months longer. But to oyster and clam with your friend Herb, son, to make certain that what we need and when we need it is in the pipeline. And forget about going back to shrimp fishing down there because the family needs for you to oyster and clam right now. But come spring you will and I do mean will be shrimp fishing up here with us where you belong whether crewing or Captaining or sweeping the dock will be decided then. Because the point is that like it or not want to or not your place is up here with us and not gallivanting all over hell and half of Georgia where you sure as hell don't belong anyway in the first place. Because I already had enough to worry about, and now I've got your loose cannon Uncle Pharoah Farrow to worry about, and on top of all that as though I didn't already have enough to worry about now I also have to live with your Mom and her worrying herself sick with worry about you still down there in that damn place where you don't belong anyway in the first place and getting yourself all wrecked up and scarred up, just look at yourself son, lordy lordy lordy just look at yourself.

So you go ahead and tell Mike that you cannot go pink shrimp fishing to the southard passed the Dry Tortugas and beyond. And you tell Mike why. But letting go of the visions of riches is not easy and you only let go of them grudgingly, because your urge to wander working on fishing boats fishing here and there and everywhere is not done. Because the mirrored sunglasses do make you mysterious and the deep tan does make you handsome and the holstered pistol does make you deadly.

But when you motion to the bartender for beers for you and Mike, he does not seem interested. So you hold up two fingers distinctly and then you point in front of you directly. But still he just stands there at the end of the bar, looking at you and then looking away and folding the bar towel and then refolding the towel and laying the towel down and then nervously picking the towel and laying the towel down and then nervously picking the towel up again. Because you and Mike have killed his evening business. So he just wants you all gone. Because in the mirror you see that all of the guys playing pool have left. So you say to the bartender, "either bring two beers, or I'll come across the bar and get them myself." Because as long as your bluff has the rednecks trembling because of what you did to Jerry Harrelson you may as well take advantage of it and enjoy it before you get found out. So the bartender finally brings the two beers.

Right away you had dismissed what Georgia McIntosh said to you the night of Johannas' party as outrageous, as unthinkable, and therefore not worth considering much less believing. But each week since just the possibility of probability has nagged at you more and more. But there is no way in hell that a day will come when there is not one commercial fisherman on any ocean on any waters, anywhere, no way in hell.

So you tell Mike what Georgia said. And you contort your

face just as she did. And you get too close to his face just as she did. And in the same harsh spitting whisper you repeat all of her words word for word and you end as she did with, "and all of you will be as dead and lifeless as the washed up marshwrack."

And Mike is as surprised as you were. And Mike is as stunned as you were. And Mikes' head and shoulders go back sharply just as yours had. And Mike says, "man, that sure doesn't sound like the Georgia McIntosh I knew growing up. Course she was several years older than me. And far too classy for any of the guys even then. But where would she hear such stuff? And start to believe such stuff? Has to be from people in Atlanta. Some people get really extreme over what they believe. And that stuff is really extreme, that's for sure. But Johanna and Georgia were water rats just like all of us. On the water every afternoon after school and weekends, racing skiffs, swimming, water skiing, just like all of us. And both of them come from long time fishing families. How could Georgia start believing such stuff. And I'm sure that Johanna doesn't know that Georgia believes such stuff. Because if Johanna knew how Georgia really feels about fisherman, that would end that friendship fast."

Then when Mike motions for two more beers, the bartender grits his teeth then shrugs his shoulders then tosses away the bar rag then goes ahead and brings the two beers, having right then reconciled himself to the fact that you all will stay until you all decide to go, having right then accepted the fact that while selling two beers isn't better than selling twenty beers it is better than selling no beers and having you all come across the bar to help yourselves to beers anyway. So Mike says, "but why would Georgia just say such stuff to you? Maybe it's because since you aren't from here you really can't retaliate against her for saying such stuff. And at the same time you can represent all the nameless faceless fishermen for her to hate as a group the way that the sports fishermen and the sea huggers hate us as a group. Because it's easier for Georgia to hate a nameless faceless group than people that she has known all of her life. So Georgia believes such stuff now. But Georgia doesn't believe such stuff enough yet to get into a fight over it. And that's how it is with the sea huggers too. They hate us and they want us off the water. But they know that we won't get off the water without a fight. But they don't yet have the stomach for a fight with us. So behind our backs while we have to keep fishing to keep our bills paid, they are busy lobbying to get all kinds of rules and regulations and restrictions passed. So that one day soon we definitely will be gone from the water."

"But Mike, groups like Greenpeace enjoy a fight as much as we do. And maybe more so. And some of their bitches are true. We are more wasteful and more destructive than is necessary. But for us it is easier and simpler and cheaper that way. So they are just reminding us of what we already know. That it really is in our best interest to not waste so much to not destroy so much. And we do get it. Finally. At least most of us do. And we will change. Too slow, yes. Too late, no. Because stubborn foot dragging doesn't warrant being run completely off the water forever. I mean get real.

155

But they are always so shrill and so extreme that you can't even talk with them."

"But Ben, all of this really goes back to twenty years ago when everyone thought that the resources didn't have limits. So the effort and the technology exploded along with the demand. But the resources were far more limited than anyone realized. But by then the effort and the technology explosion was already exploding. And there just isn't any way to stop an explosion once the explosion has started, once the boom is going BBOOOMM. All that can be done is to wait for the last m in BBooomm, then pick up the pieces of whatever is left and then go on from there with better controls better management."

Because fishermen really enjoy talking about fishing even more than fishermen enjoy talking about sex and fishermen thoroughly enjoy talking about sex. So as you and Mike get further caught up in the excitement of this really good fishing conversation your beer drinking increases in speed and therefore volume. So the bartender takes it upon himself to bring you all two more beers before you all are quite ready for them because in your conversation excitement he sees a chance to recoup some of his recent beer sales losses due to the sudden patron quantity reduction of which you and Mike were directly responsible. So you say, "I understand all that, Mike, and I agree with you, but things have happened on land too that have impacted the resources just as much as over-fishing. Because coastal development loses habitat. Because polluting rivers pollutes the sea. So there's plenty of blame to go around, why just target us?"

And Mike answers, "because we're the easy target because we're the most visible target. Because there we are, all the boats out bobbing on the water and pulling nets at crawl speed for everyone and his brother to see. But smokestacks and drainpipes can be camouflaged. And clearing and draining and filling can creep along so it is hardly noticed. But there we are silhouetted against the horizon like a whore in church wearing a red dress. But there are a lot fewer of us silhouetted there on the horizon than there were. Because very few new boats are being built. So the lost boats aren't being replaced. Just look at what has happened during the months that you have been down here. Slicer loses Sea Warrior. You and Forrest lose Mustang. You and I lose Silly Sally. And that's just here locally. Fishing boats are regularly being lost everywhere. But few of them will be replaced. And Slicer will never Captain another boat. And Forrest is God knows where, and he probably will never fish again. So out of four fishermen here locally, only you and I are still fishing. And this same thing is going on everywhere."

Then the front door is suddenly pushed open. And I'll be damned if it isn't Georgia McIntosh big as life coming in with the same girlfriend from before coming in behind her. And you look in the bar mirror and say, "oh lordy lordy, Mike, look who's here." And Mike looks in the mirror and says, "well I'll be damned, speak of the devil." Then Mike laughs and says, "just remember, Ben, there's a fine line between love and hate." And right away Georgia recognizes you sitting there at the bar and she looks at you hard hard and she shakes her head grim grim.   Then she and her girlfriend go on and begin to rack the balls at a pool table. And the bartender grins like he is chewing tacks because of the unexpected business.   But your head has become light once again.   And the same something is going thump bump in your chest.   Because once again and as always Georgia McIntosh is so blonde beautiful and so clothes sophisticated. So you say, "oh lordy lordy, I never learn." Because you see your hand reaching for a quarter among the beer change on the bar to go put on the pool table rail for winners.

CHAPTER 16

So you say, "lordy lordy lordy, that's a cold-assed wind, "outloud to yourself. Having already begun to routinely talk to yourself as most bay fishermen do, whether crabber or clammer or oysterer or scalloper, for the comfort of it for the reassurance of it out here in a skiff all alone on the water all day with only yourself and your whichever harvesting work for company good and dependable and loyal company though they are but talking to yourself just makes them better company it really does.

And it is a cold-assed damn February wind indeed that only yesterday had blown loud down and along the high raw plains far up to the northwest that today shivers coastal Georgia until it has withdrawn within itself. But neither rain nor sleet nor cold nor dark of night stays the courier from his appointed rounds, or some such bullshit, or sturdy bay fisherman either for that matter, or so they are quick to boast while thumping their hairy chests. So here you are knee-deep wet in boggy mud picking oysters and shivering and wondering what the hell you are doing out here while Herb is toasty warm in the cab of his raggedy old truck somewhere on I95 south hauling a load of oysters to a shucking house in St. Augustine. But it really isn't too bad as long as you keep busy because you are dressed warm in layers for it so only your hands and your feet and your face are numb. So you straighten from bending over picking and you rub your hands together inside the thick gloves and you say burrrr and you see your breath cloud saying burrrr in sympathy for your numb hands and feet and face. But your foul weather coat stops the wind from blowing inward to numb your core. And with the hood up and by standing with your back to it, the wind can only swirl by and whisper whoooo as it passes.

So you are a solitary figure indeed standing here on the one thousand acre mudflat in Mud River that is Herbs' prime oyster beds. And prime the beds are now and primer still the beds will become as long as Herb can continue to evade bankruptcy, delicate balancing act that that is as all who have performed it while dancing delicately will say a hearty amen brother to. Because cluster oysters are the stepchild oyster with all of the natural obstacles to overcome. Because single oysters grow on firm bottom like first born heirs pampered and lazy and preordained. But cluster oysters grow on the silty bog that will quickly smother them. So cluster oysters grow up and out and away and any direction or configuration except down into the smothering silty bog. So they grow long and they grow wide and they grow fast with big pearly meats inside their thin thin shells that are as sharp and as deadly as the deadliest sharp sword. So they grow wildly and desperately and frantically and tenaciously and heroically for the several years of their very short stepchild lives. Because besides doing the best that they can to anchor the silty bog in place, which usually is a losing battle in the long run anyway, their main reason for existence after perpetuating their kind which they do very well indeed is as food for all the other sea and shore critters. Food! Food! Gnash, gnash, gnash! Here I come and I will eat you if I can so you better watch out. So you would grow wildly and desperately and frantically and tenaciously and heroically too.

But Herb really has done marvelously well with his proper management of this resource that was so long neglected before he came. But since coming he has had to overcome the usual bureaucratic being dumped on endlessly and being harassed to destruction that so stifles so many young businesses that already have enough to overcome as it is without bureaucrats further stifling them with good intentions that are void of common sense. Because Herb has single handily and in spite of everything tripled the size of these beds in only the several years of his pulling down the beds twice a year so that the oysters are forced to begin again but this time begin on a firmer foundation and with the old dead shell weeded out as any proper farmer would weed his fields so that the coming generations of oysters will be less cluttered and better scattered and absolutely charged with vitality. So that we humans will rush to join with the other critters in saying gnash gnash here I come and I will eat you if I can.

And Herb does give his customers a good bushel of oysters. Because as he says just pick a bushel like you would like to get if you were the customer. But there is a lot of work in culling down these stepchild cluster oysters to a good singles and doubles and triples bushel. But the twice daily seawater flush that they get this far from the highlands makes them salty real salty and plump and pristine so one taste and they sell themselves so maybe one day these Mud River oysters will be as famous as Blue Point oysters. But if the Florida and Louisiana bootleggers don't stop harvesting in polluted waters causing so many people to get sick and some to die, then everyone will just stop eating oysters. Then look at how much will be lost as the baby will be thrown out with the bathwater Herb included. But the reality is that Herbs' bankruptcy is being postponed because of extraordinary circumstances. Because for now and until spring when oyster sales slow to an almost stop anyway for the summer, your Dad and your Uncle Pharoah Farrow are trading quantity for quality from six hundred miles away as is the St. Augustine shucker from half that distance when usually they would expect both quality and quantity plus less freight costs for their maximum profit. And because you pick for Herb as he picks for himself. But Herb does not have any local support never has had never will have so Mike bottom lined it when he said, 'theres' no way in hell that Herb is going to build a successful shellfish business down here.' And right or wrong, fair or not does not matter. And all the bitching and the moaning in the world until the cows come home even will not change that. So that is the end of that conversation yes it is.

But you really have gotten into this oyster picker clam digger thing, this bay fisherman thing. You didn't realize how noisy and crowded and impersonal that trawler fishing is until recently. And while you love that work life and you miss that work life, this alone on a skiff on the water all day is a good worklife too. So maybe when you get back home in the spring you will lease some bottom and see if you can't get an oyster and clam farm going up there in Core Sound near Sealevel and Atlantic. Because you no longer take the resources here for granted as you once did. Because Georgia McIntosh certainly got your attention about that. Yes hell she did. And yes hell she will get your attention about other things too when she comes home soon to visit. Because who would have thought that you and Georgia together was possible?

But, again, you are sure that you hear someone hollering hello to you from far away. So, again, you straighten from bending over the mounded beds picking oysters. But with the tide out you are surrounded by one hundred yards of mudflat in every direction. To the north the oyster beds and the mudflat just go on and on until finally ending at where Sapelo Sound is about to become Sapelo Inlet. There is the woods line on the backside of Sapelo Island to the east several hundred yards away with a narrow strip of shelly marsh and then a shallow water channel between it and this dried out mudflat. But you do not see anyone in that direction either. And to the south there is only the spartina grass marsh that just goes on and on to the horizon. So you look to the west and there is your dried out skiff sitting on the dried out mudflat that goes for a hundred yards before the start of the deepwater channel that swings wide and hugs the Eagle Creek Island side of Mud River in that direction. But you do not see anyone. But you hear the far way hello again. And looking lower down right on the waterline you do see three separate arms waving from three separate upper bodies there right on the water line in the middle of the deepwater channel. So you climb the mounded oyster bed and sure enough there in the distance are three waving arms from three upper bodies that are sitting in three separate kayaks. So you cup your thickly gloved hands near your mouth and you holler hello back. Then you wave big back. Then the three arms wave again and you hear three far away hellos coming from that far away. Then the three kayakers just continue on their solitary journey south. So you stand on the high mounded oysters and you watch them until they are no longer in sight. And you wonder why they are out kayaking on such a cold February windy day. Then you remember that fair weather sports fisherman are not out tearing around in their speed boats hauling ass and burning gas on raw days such as this. So today is a perfect day to kayak these timeless estuary waters and to appreciate their pristine beauty.

And from up here you can see the five bushels of oysters that you have already picked in the red mesh bags setting upright in your skiff. And even though the tide has already turned and started in at the Inlet, it will be well over an hour before this huge mudflat begins to flood. Then it will be awhile longer before there is enough water under your skiff so you can leave. Because with six to eight foot tides normal down here one hell of a lot of water goes and comes in a tide, it surely does. But there is still plenty of time for you to pick several more bushels.

But as you step down from the mound, that part of the mound gives way. The mud and the silt and the terribly clustered and aimed in every direction and sharp as the sharpest deadly sword oysters just give way. So your feet begin to go out from under you. So you begin to sit down hard to fall down hard. But for this once you ignore your sea instinct that in all falls at sea you always bring your hands to your body to protect your hands at all costs, and let your body bear the brunt of the fall because it can better withstand it. So you do the land instinct reaction, and you put your hands down to break your fall.

But right away your thick gloves are horribly sliced by the sword edged oysters. Then right away your hands from your palms to beyond your wrists are horribly sliced by the sword edged oysters. And right away you know that you have been killed. And in that instant you know that this is true. Just as you know that your error in judgment is true. Just as you know that you have done what you know absolutely to not do is true. Because in a sea crisis reacting quickly can be learned. But reacting correctly you either do or else you do not do. You cannot learn that. So the hundreds of times that you have reacted quickly and correctly do not count now do not matter now are by the boards now. Because for this once you reacted quickly but you reacted incorrectly. And as always in a sea crisis, there are no second chances.

And with the shredded gloves off you see the horrible damage done. And right away you know that, yes, you have been killed. Because both of your wrists are horribly slashed many times passed the muscles and the tendons to the bone and almost to your forearms. And your blood is pumping out and your blood is squirting out and you blood is flowing out. And your hands do not work when you try to clasp them around your wrists to try to at least slow the horrible blood loss. Hands that have always worked so swiftly so very well, now do not work at all. And you have already begun to feel faint. And you are all alone. And no one will come. And it will be well over an hour before the tide floats your dried out on the mudflat skiff so you can leave which now you cannot leave. So the door has been slammed shut. So there is no way out, no, not this time. But all the other sea crisis times there was always someway, anyway, out. But this time there is no way out this time. So you have been killed indeed. And now you are just going through the last minutes of dying.

So Georgia was right. Because you will be as dead and lifeless as the washed up marshwrack. Because the incoming tide will float dead you from here. Then the currents and the swirls within the tide will begin collecting all of the dead floating spartina grass and the drink jugs and the beer cans and the drifting wood and all of the other debre including dead you. And at high tide it will have all of this marshwrack collected into a raft beside the marsh where the outgoing tide will leave it. Because the sea is a tidy housekeeper when left to herself.

So Herb was right. Because down here will surely get you if you don't watch out. Yes hell it will. But you really do not mind becoming food now for all of the critters. Because after all of the hundreds of tons of them that you have harvested, now it is time for you to give back. So this is fair. So this is proper. So this is just.

But you see that the pumping and the squirting have almost stopped. But the flowing continues though more slowly now. So it will not be very long now. And the expression on your Moms' face that appears before you is one of sudden horror and shocked disbelief that she that she would do this to you so soon again. So you show your Mom your wrists. But she cannot kiss them and make them better. No, not this time. So you say, "Mom." But already your voice sounds distant. Because she that she wants you home with her. And you do not refuse the sea.

www.ingramcontent.com/pod-product-compliance
Lightning Source LLC
Chambersburg PA
CBHW060403030726
47497CB00003B/828